SIDE EFFECTS MAY VARY

What if the cure is worse than the disease?

ELLIS REID

Copyright © 2016 Ellis Reid
All rights reserved.

ISBN: 1534830014
ISBN 13: 9781534830011

For you,
You have always been in my heart and have walked with me every step of the way.

Part One

Chapter 1

An extract taken from an international online newspaper called InterNewsOnline:

NEW WONDER DRUG RELEASED WORLD-WIDE
By Jodie Fisher **Monday 15 March 2032**

Doctors and scientists all over the globe are hailing the latest treatment to hit the market as a "wonder drug."

The cure for Alzheimer's, called "AZ," is deemed to be the most successful cure of all time and was developed by the Kingston-based pharmaceutical company Medipharm Inc. It is available to patients today and claims to reverse the damage to the brain caused by Alzheimer's disease.

Developers of the new drug claim that it can permanently reverse the damage that Alzheimer's has inflicted.

AZ is taken once, orally. Carers will notice that patients who have taken the drug appear to start the improvement process within one month—although overall improvement, to the point where the patient is considered safe to resume his or her old life unassisted, is a long process. For example, studies have shown that a person who has been diagnosed with Alzheimer's for three years will take a further three years, after taking the drug, to regain all aspects of his or her life before the disease caused the damage. While this is fairly accurate for most cases, each patient is individual in his or her recovery time and in recovery symptoms.

In a statement on Medipharm Inc.'s website, neuroscientist and professor Saanvi Singh claimed that the new drug would be "phenomenally successful" and "would change the entire world and the existence of the human race."

Since its inception in 2015, Professor Saanvi Singh has been at the forefront of the drug's development. She went on to explain that "AZ targets the damaged nerve cells and brain tissue that have been destroyed by the disease. In simple terms, it cleans and repairs the neurones and restores total functionality to the patient. After a matter of years, the patient's condition is completely reversed. They are able to walk, talk, and think exactly as they had before. With no risk of the disease returning. In each of our human trials, the evidence shows that AZ wipes Alzheimer's disease completely off the map of the human brain."

The drug underwent extensive trials on mice in the United Kingdom before going onto several rounds of human trials in the URSA in 2025. In the second batch of animal trials, the scientists tested on five hundred mice, recording their progress in a series of "memory" tests. They then took a second set of information after the drug was administered to three hundred of the mice; the other two hundred were not given the drug. The inoculated mice displayed better memory skills and were more likely to understand the tasks set for them.

They had a 99 per cent success rate in the tests they were set, compared to a 15 per cent success rate of the mice that went without the treatment. Although the mice did not have Alzheimer's, the drug improved their memories and overall performance, which led scientists to believe that the drug could be applied to those who had the disease, with successful results.

Human trials started in 2025, and the results were staggering. Most of the trial patients explained that the entire experience was like "coming out of a really long coma." Many expressed their excitement over their second lease on life. The United Kingdom's Alzheimer's Disease Association (ADA) and the NHS have set up a free counselling and rehabilitation service for patients who wish to take the drug. Other countries have set up similar support networks.

Family members were emotional as they listened to the announcement this morning: "We're completely overwhelmed. My father was diagnosed in 2026 when he was sixty-three, and at the time, we were distraught because back then it was considered a death sentence. We know it will take a while for the drug to repair the damage, but we can't wait to have him back," Dexter Harper, whose father, Adam Harper, is an Alzheimer's sufferer, told us today. They are scheduled to receive treatment for Adam in the next two weeks.

Many people have questioned the necessity of the drug, stating by the time the Alzheimer's sufferers have been fully cured of the illness, they are too old to continue with their previous healthy lifestyles. Some are saying that the sufferer may even be happier without the drug and wish to continue with the deterioration.

Others are claiming that with the emergence of this drug, the human population will skyrocket. They believe that diseases are important to control the population level and eliminating these diseases through cures could be catastrophic to the environment and to those living in poverty already.

Critic Marina Baker wrote in response to the drug's release: "With each elimination of a disease, a new one replaces it. We cured Ebola, and then the Zika virus appeared. We found cures for cancer…those cancers became more aggressive, and our cures couldn't cope. How long will it be before a new, more deadly, and far more terrifying disease falls upon the human race? And what if we never find a cure for that one?"

Chapter 2

Three years later
March 2035

"Good evening. I'm Michelle March, and you are watching *The March Show*, live. As always, tonight I'll be bringing you an hour of discussion and comment on the most current news stories," the presenter began. Her chemically whitened teeth drew a person's eyes quite sharply to her mouth whenever she spoke. The whiteness of them was so pure that it made whoever was watching her self-consciously run their tongues across their own teeth to check for blemishes.

Despite the fact that she was nearing fifty-five years of age, Michelle March looked good. Her platinum-blonde hair, cut in a neat bob, fell around her angular jawline. The wrinkles that framed her strikingly cold and grey eyes were the only feature to reveal the secret of her age. The rest of her face recalled a time when she had been the object of men's desire. Once, she had been the poster girl of the decade.

Eight consecutive years at the top of laddish magazines objectifying "hot 100" rankings. Today, she was on the verge of a reluctant retirement, still considered beautiful but no longer desired or envied.

As she spoke, her film crew stared straight ahead, their eyes unseeing, their concentration wandering. Her cameraperson idly picked his nose and ate the findings as he slouched against the railing behind him. Had Michelle been a little less self-involved, she would have interpreted their lack of interest as a sign that her time in television was over.

And it *was* over, but Michelle had never been one to leave quietly.

"This month marks the third anniversary that AZ, the cure for Alzheimer's disease, became available worldwide. Three years on, we look at the effects of the drug on society and discuss how successful the drug has been.

"Joining me on the sofa today is Desi Ezra, the director of the hit documentary series that followed the lives of Alzheimer's sufferers on their path of recovery. We're also joined by the United Kingdom's health minister, Mona Strauss, and finally Jana Duke, whose father was given the drug during the trials and who has become quite the success story."

The camera cut to each guest as they were introduced. Desi, more comfortable behind the camera than in front, gave a sheepish smile, her head slightly bowed. Mona Strauss, ever the politician, flashed an award-winning Cheshire cat's smile at the camera, a smile that did not reach her eyes. And finally, a plain-faced Jana Duke gave a grimace in response to her own name. Beads of sweat had begun to appear on her brow.

"So, Desi, let's start with you!" Michelle leaned forward, her mouth spread eagerly into a smile bearing those pearly white teeth. The effect reminded Desi of a crocodile, and she took an instinctive shuffle back into her seat; the action went unnoticed by Michelle.

Desi was polite but quiet; in rehearsals, the volume of her microphone had had to be jacked up to twice the level of the other interviewees. But despite its lack of power, Jana felt entranced by Desi's voice.

Before the show had started, Jana had overheard Desi and Mona exchanging suggestions of new TV shows to watch. Desi's voice had commanded respect, and the fact that it was so low in volume only made Jana want to lean in to listen harder.

Jana listened now and waited patiently; her time would come. She made a conscious effort neither to check her watch nor to check the clock that hung at the back of the studio. Five minutes passed.

And then ten.

And then thirty minutes.

And then forty.

Until finally it was her turn to speak.

"Jana! Wow, am I excited to speak to you! You bet. I hope my other visitors don't mind when I say that I have saved the best 'til last."

Jana shifted uncomfortably in her seat. She had a heightened awareness of the fact that this happy and chipper version of Michelle was a far cry from the one just before the cameras started to roll.

Stay calm, not yet, not yet. Don't lose it, she thought to herself as she forced a tight-lipped smile.

"So, your father, Aaron, he suffered from Alzheimer's for four years, am I right?"

"Yeah, it was about that—"

"What an awful time for you and your family. Though I must say, you're looking very well tonight. Doesn't Jana look fabulous?" Michelle crowed at her audience. "And your father, he received the cure…? What was that like?"

"He was actually in one of the original UK trials before the drug became available—"

"That's fantastic! Isn't that right, folks?" Michelle turned her crocodile smile to the audience, and Jana felt an overwhelming wave of hatred, plunging her skin into a hot flush. "Desi, you've actually met Aaron, and you followed part of his story during his recovery, didn't you?"

The limelight switched to Desi, who had gained more confidence as the interview progressed. She nodded enthusiastically and moved forward in her seat. She explained how much of Aaron's story she had already learnt by making the documentary.

"Now, Jana, let's get back to you. Can you tell us a bit more about Aaron? How's he coping? He's been declared as completely cured, hasn't he?"

"Yes, yes, he has. I'm glad that you—"

"That's fantastic news, isn't it, ladies and gents?" Michelle turned to the audience yet again, her crocodile smile not reaching her eyes. There were woops and cheers from the audience. "So what's Aaron up to now? I've been told he's back at work."

The room was buzzing with excitement; Jana could feel it. The mood appeared to be good, and why wouldn't it be? As far as everybody was aware, Alzheimer's had been cured, and it didn't exist as a threat anymore. That was certainly something to be pleased about.

"He's not at work—" Jana began.

Michelle let out a hoot of laughter, drowning the rest of Jana's sentence. "Well, who can blame him? We all love a little holiday, don't we? Ha-ha!" Michelle reached out and gave Desi's leg a light slap of jubilation. Jana noticed Desi's flinch in response.

Jana could feel her blood beginning to boil. She wasn't sure if she could take one more interruption from this woman. She had come here with one job to do, and this stupid bitch wouldn't stop cutting her off. Bracing her back against the rigidity of the sofa, she decided to give herself one last push.

"*Actually*," Jana began again, her voice a little louder than she had anticipated. The sudden rise in volume made Desi on the couch next to her jump. Jana's microphone let out a squawk of distaste. "Actually, he is not at work. He's in a coma."

For those viewing the show from the comfort of their own homes, they would be forgiven for not noticing the fractional expression of surprise in Michelle's face. However, sitting alongside her, time slowed down in the studio, and Jana witnessed the momentary crease of Michelle's brow.

⌁

Michelle stalled momentarily as she wracked her brain for more information. The prompts she had been given before the start of the show hadn't mentioned anything about a coma. She mentally replayed the rehearsal they had earlier in the day; Jana's semi-scripted response wasn't anything like this one.

She was meant to say that Aaron wasn't at work but had taken an early retirement. She was meant to go on and explain that he had developed a fantastic relationship with his new grandchildren. It was meant to be the happy ending that the audience had been waiting for; the credits would roll to the soundtrack of cheers.

"A coma? Well that is unusual…" Michelle's mind was in overdrive. Where did Jana expect this to lead? How could she coax her back onto the script? Was her producer listening? Had they already cut the live feed out of the studio?

"It's not that unusual. In fact, if you…" Jana began again. Michelle noticed the slight pinking of Jana's cheeks and the shaking of her hands as she spoke. "If you go back and look at all of the trial cases of AZ, you will see that everybody else who took the drug in that trial period is either in a coma or they are dead."

A gasp rippled through the audience. Michelle could see that Jana had had her desired effect, and the crowd were listening now. Through the tension, Michelle became suddenly conscious of her producer's voice screaming down her earpiece.

"Get her out of there. Get back to Desi!" the producer shouted.

Michelle's crocodile smile did not waver. "Well, Jana, I'm sure that's not true. There are always one or two side effects, but for the most part, the trials have been completely successful." Michelle let out an awkward laugh.

"That's a fucking lie, and you know it. Look it up! AZ is killing people, and nobody gives a damn. It's all being hidden and—" There was an electrical screech as Jana's microphone was abruptly switched off, and the camera switched back to a panicked Desi.

The crowd in front of them began to boo at Jana; the sound of their upset spurred Michelle to go on. She could feel them on her side.

"Please don't swear on my show, Jana. We're before the watershed here, darling." Michelle winked at the camera and let out another one of her fake laughs. "For our audience at home, I'm ever so sorry."

Michelle rotated her head back to Jana with the slowness of a predator that has just realised where its prey is.

"And, darling, I would appreciate it if you wouldn't spread malicious lies in an attempt to panic my viewers. Mona, let's see what you make of this. You've seen the figures…" Michelle prompted the politician.

Mona seized her opportunity and leaned forward eagerly. "Well, the figures speak for themselves. Any claims of patients dying are completely unfounded, and people spreading these kinds of lies are causing undue distress. Thousands of patients took part in those trials, and they have all been highly effective. There is no evidence of negative side effects such as comas or death."

Jana's voice, weak in the vast expanse of the studio, was still being picked up by Desi's microphone. It could still be heard between the breaks in Mona's speech.

"Comas aren't the worst…AZ is a deadly virus…I'm trying to warn you all…a cover-up…"

"*And* that's all we've got time for," Michelle half shouted. "Thanks very much to our panel today and for our audience and to our viewers at home. Goodnight from me, and it's goodnight from Desi Ezra, Mona Strauss, and Jana Duke."

The crowd let out a huge applause as the credits rolled across the screen. Michelle, still conscious of her audience, nodded to Jana.

"Come with me, sweetheart. Let's talk about this some more in a little privacy," she offered, keeping her tone neutral.

Outside the studio and out of sight of the public, Michelle led Jana straight into the path of two burly security guards.

They snatched at her and dragged her towards the maintenance elevator.

"Who the fuck let this girl in here? Whose fucking idea was it to have her on my fucking show?" Michelle screamed at anybody close enough to listen. "Did nobody think to do a fucking background check? Whoever is responsible for this, I want them in my dressing room right fucking now, and they can kiss goodbye ever working with me again."

Jana was ejected from the building and onto the street with a force that sent her sprawling onto the ground. The studio doors slammed shut behind her. She stumbled to her feet, furious and dejected that her plan had failed and that Michelle's loyal audience had chosen not to listen to her.

That night, she returned home to her father and cried over his lifeless body, his skin pale and sallow, deep, dark hollows carving out shadows around his eyelids.

The next day, Jana's medical history was leaked online. Forged documents citing that she had undergone periods of "psychiatric involvement" appeared on the Internet. Jana refused to believe that it was a coincidence that this false information appeared only twelve hours after she crossed Michelle March. The forged files had their desired effect, though, and any credibility that she might have gained through her speech on *The March Show* was extinguished overnight.

Later that year, as she packed up a small case of things to move away from the city, she recalled her time on Michelle March's show. She had expected the revelation to be easy, that the hard part—getting onto the show—was over. She had expected some people to ignore her, but she had also expected a movement of some kind. She had even anticipated Michelle being on her side, that Michelle might give her a platform on which she could tell the public the truth. Something that they all deserved to know. She had hoped that the interview on Michelle's show might ignite a spark of doubt nationwide, but her plan had backfired.

But then, who would listen to a girl like Jana anyway? She was an unknown. She had come across as hysterical, and she had underestimated the loyalty of Michelle's viewers. Jana had been portrayed as the bully.

That summer, as she rooted through drawers, she watched Michelle March's live coverage outside a hospital in Edinburgh. The strapline at the bottom of the screen stated "deadly outbreak of virus in Scottish hospital," and on that particular humid day in June, the story was considered "breaking."

Jana rolled her eyes and thought to herself that it was probably far too late for all of these news outlets to be showing an interest now, particularly *The March Show*, which had framed her as a pariah in the weeks following her outburst on live TV.

Yes, it was probably far too late. The damage, from their inability to publicise the mutation of the virus, was done. And the viewers who turned their attention to other more intensely publicised and intensely mundane stories were already doomed.

When the live feed abruptly terminated and her computer screen, on which she had been viewing the report, went black, she panicked. Until she reminded herself that she had tried to forewarn everyone, had tried to persuade them all to prepare themselves, but they had not listened.

Chapter 3

Four years earlier
May 3031

Mornings had never been my strong suit; my wife could tell you that. It didn't matter how much sleep I had had the night before. It was still a struggle to make that first step out of bed.

On days when my wife felt particularly kind, she would find the biggest mug in the kitchen, fill it with hot coffee, and place it on the cabinet next to the bed we had shared for a large portion of our lives.

On these days, the steaming mug of hot coffee made waking up a little bit easier but only fractionally. I couldn't tell you what it was that made me so reluctant to get out of bed. I only know that I'd always been like that, even before I was an adult. The only thing that had changed since then was that when I was a child, instead of the enticing scent of the freshly made brew, it was my mother's threats about taking me back to "the home" that would drag me from my nest of duvets and pillows.

"The home" of course didn't exist, at least not in the sense that she meant. But I only realised that when I grew a little older and a little wiser to her threats.

As a child, "the home" meant the place that my adoptive parents found me and rescued me from. I never learnt the specifics of it, but my imagination was vivid enough to make me believe that it was a place where the staff beat you and the children stole your food and your toys. In reality, it probably wasn't like that at all. But by that age I had watched enough TV to come to the most dramatic conclusion of all.

Don't get me wrong. My mother was lovely. She was kind, she was generous, and most of all she was always there for me, as was my father. They had always been honest right from the start about how I had been brought into their lives. They were never ones to shy away from the truth. So you might think it mean when I tell you about these morning exchanges, when my mother hollered and threatened me until I rolled out of bed, but they were necessary.

I see now that she was exasperated and exhausted because her one and only child refused to budge from under the covers. What she said to me on those mornings was hollow, and she hadn't meant a word of it. And besides, I was old enough to know full well that adopted kids didn't just get "returned."

My parents were model people. They went to church on Sundays, were always polite, and whenever Mum baked, she always made extra to take into work the next day.

The same could not be said for my biological parents, who didn't bother to contact me until I was married and had a child of my own. Maybe they had their reasons and maybe they thought those reasons were good. But, and you'll have to excuse the cliché, all my life I had felt abandoned, and their lame attempts to get in contact with me thirty years after they gave me up was not enough for me to want to forge a bond with them. I forgave them, though, and I told them as much. But the thing with forgiveness is that it doesn't ever really erase the pain; it just numbs it a little.

For some reason, I woke up earlier than Lois on one grey morning in May, despite the fact that for our entire relationship, she had always been the first to rise. But I guess there's an exception to every rule. I made my own coffee and sat at the kitchen table. It was a heavy, round oak piece that was positioned in the middle of the room. Lois and I had purchased it together a few years ago from a family-run furniture shop on the outskirts of town.

I loved the table and often when I sat at it, I pictured the romantic meals that Lois and I had shared together in the most recent part of our marriage. I recalled the heated arguments we had around it and the even more heated make-up sex we had moments later. No matter what I thought about, that table never failed to make me smile, eventually. There were enough good memories to vastly outweigh the bad, enough to always remind me that we had a great marriage.

Often when I was finished reminiscing over the table and all the memories attached, I would sneak a glance at the wide stove that spanned across half of one of the kitchen walls. At that stove was where we had our first dinner together in our new home. Then my eyes would flick over to the chair opposite me. That chair was where Lois sat when I suggested that we should have a baby. A tiny baby, crying and laughing and gurgling away. Jessie.

Then I was back to thinking about that table again. Funny how attached I was to that big hunk of wood, but I couldn't help it. Psychology predicts that after my biological parents rejected me, I should have struggled with attachment, but that couldn't be farther from the truth. I loved everything I ever set eyes on, and I loved it fiercely. And if you asked Lois, it was probably not one of my most redeeming features. She tended to want to blitz the house periodically and throw a lot of things out, but I would cling to each and every item in that black bin bag and beg for it to be kept. I was a hoarder and probably would have been much worse had Lois not put her foot down.

My attachment to the table wasn't completely unmerited. After all, that table was where I sat when I broke the news that I was finally pregnant.

I had looked across at Lois and taken her hands, and it had been nearly impossible for me to stifle the grin that kept poking the corners of my mouth upwards. Even now when

I think about it, I find it hard to stop my face from erupting into that tell-all smile.

I had been beyond excited, but I had been careful too. I had taken a minimum of ten pregnancy tests earlier that day, all of which had turned out to be positive. Those tests had elated me even more because now I knew with certainty that I was expecting a baby with the woman I loved. You could say I had every right to be excited and had every right to that uncontrollable grin on my face.

But our excitement didn't last for long. The little bubble we coasted along in popped a few months later. I guess we had an idea about what might happen before it even popped. Call it mother's intuition, doubled. The initial happiness that overwhelmed us at the beginning had quickly turned to fear, an unconscious uneasiness that only came to a couple that knew something wasn't quite right about this one.

In the beginning, we had dismissed the idea of discussing names because it was "too soon," and we had been right. A month or two after we sat in the kitchen, I began to bleed. It had taken Lois weeks to get the stain out of the hallway carpet after that particular incident. After a while, Lois had the carpet removed completely. Although a visitor could barely decipher the stain on the dark carpet, the mere memory was enough for us. And seeing it each time we entered the house became unbearable. It was a constant reminder we were doing something wrong. Somewhere along the line, we had misread the script of our lives, and we were being punished for it.

It took about six months for us to build up our courage to make the second attempt. But that initial uneasiness and fear never left. It was only a matter of weeks, that time, before I lost our second baby. I couldn't tell you how we coped with that second loss, and when I look back, it feels like that part of our lives was just a big black cloud. I can't tell you how our relationship managed to withstand such heartbreak; I can only tell you that somehow, some way, we found the strength to deal with it, and we tried a third time.

Maybe we unconsciously promised each other that this would be the final attempt, and maybe the universe saw so clearly how ready we were to give up that it finally granted our wish.

The third time, well, I suppose that after the first and second tries have failed, there becomes an unwritten law in which hopes are forbidden to be attended to. The tiny spark that simmered away at the bottom of my heart remained desperately forgotten about, until after eight months without complication, we finally ventured out of the house to buy our baby's first item of clothing.

A Babygro, brown, with little paws for socks and gloves and a hood with long floppy rabbit ears stitched to the top. It was the cutest thing you had ever seen, and I'm sure that even in Lois's most obsessive throw-everything-away mood, she would not have parted with it. Since Jessie had grown out of it now, it had probably made its way into the great unknown expanse that was our attic.

Before that purchase, Lois had been absolutely unbearable to live with. She itched to plan, to purchase, and to paint the baby's potential room. Lois without a plan was like a cat without whiskers; she just wasn't herself. It had been practically impossible for her to sit around and wait. If it had been up to me, I wouldn't have bought a single thing for Jessie until I held her in my arms.

"Third time lucky," our midwife had said and our family and friends had cautiously joked. And I had prayed to whatever god existed that it really would be just that.

Jessie was born on Monday 16 March 2015. It had been surprisingly warm for early spring, but there had been no wind or rain, and there had been a hint of summer in the air. I can still picture that. The sky had been bright blue, not a cloud in sight, and I could feel the sun just wishing to make its full strength known to the world.

Lois had been reluctantly called into work that day, something about a shortage of staff, so I had been left by myself to clean the house. It was a compulsive habit that had sprung up in my final trimester, and it hadn't come naturally to me. Yet I loved doing it. When I went into labour, I snatched up my bag and drove myself to the hospital as soon as the pains kicked in. We weren't friendly with our neighbours for some reason or other, and I wasn't able to reach Lois. So I left a voicemail.

After two hours of no word from her, she arrived suddenly with an apology, the biggest bunch of flowers I had ever seen, and a small blue teddy bear. Both had been purchased from one of the few shops in the hospital foyer on her way in. Jessie carried that soft toy around with her everywhere.

That was almost three years ago, and Jessie was big now. She had sprouted teeth and was answering back. Much to my dismay, that girl had made it clear that she didn't have a problem with early mornings, a trait she must have inherited from Lois.

That was when I realised that it struck me as odd that it was gone 6:00 a.m. and I hadn't heard a sound from Jessie yet. Normally she was wide awake and hollering for her breakfast at that time of the day. Then again, my head would normally be buried under a stack of pillows at that time of day too, so something had definitely upset the status quo somewhere. I didn't give Jessie's sleeping habits too much thought after that. I told myself to enjoy the silence while it lasted and make another cup of coffee. In any case, I was fairly sure it was Lois's turn to tend to our daughter.

It was when I started to make that second cup of coffee that I ran into my first problem. I couldn't find anything.

I loved my wife, but sometimes her ever-obsessive behaviour drove me absolutely mad. If I left something on the kitchen counter for longer than a few minutes, she would scold me and recite her mantra, "Everything has its own place." And, yes, everything did have its own place, but that was precisely my problem. For once, I wanted a set of keys to stay off the hook. I *wanted* to wander around the house aimlessly looking for something I had misplaced. I couldn't do that in this house except for right then—and in the months that followed, but I'll get to that later.

I opened the fridge and looked for the milk and found the jar of coffee in there instead. Everything did have its own place, but its place was meant to be logical. And a jar of dried goods in a fridge didn't seem logical to me. That's when something started to feel wrong. I got this buzzing feeling in my gut and a nervousness that I couldn't explain yet. That happened often in those days, that nagging feeling that clawed at the back of my mind.

Footsteps came softly down the stairs and distracted me from my train of thought, and a moment later, Lois appeared in the kitchen doorway. I wondered how she had managed to make it downstairs without waking Jessie. Jessie who had the supersonic hearing that only a toddler could have.

The stark light of the kitchen shone onto Lois's face as she paused in the doorway. Despite how early it was, she looked beautiful, but with some reluctance, I'll admit that I thought she looked a little old too, but mostly beautiful. Maybe the early-morning wake-up-calls from our child were starting to take their toll on her. I held up my empty mug.

"Coffee?" I asked, but she shook her head. As I turned my back on her to tend to the kettle, I noticed her shoulders slump a little, and she released a sigh.

"Hey, why don't you come back to bed? It's a little early, don't you think?" she asked, her voice weary. Her words cracked as they came out, her voice not used to being employed at this time in the morning. She rubbed at her blue eyes roughly. A messy bun of auburn hair sat on top of her head. A few strands had worked themselves loose at the base of her neck. I fought an urge to layer kisses where those loose curls were.

"I've got work in a few hours," I reminded her. "Will you check on Jessie? She's not woken up yet, and she'll probably want breakfast soon." I added, remembering again that Jessie should have been awake by now. I busied myself with the kettle and tried to pretend I knew where I had put the milk. If the coffee was in the fridge, then the milk would be in the...cupboard?

Lois sighed a second time.

"She doesn't have to go to school today."

"Huh? Why would she have to go to school anyway? She's three." I laughed and waited for Lois to join me. But I heard her breath catch in her throat. I ignored it; she was looking for an argument again, making up pointless reasons to make me feel awful. My good mood felt like it was fading fast. "I need to shower and get ready for work. Will you just check on Jessie, please?"

There was a pause as Lois took a deep breath. As ever, she made no effort to contain her exasperation. My skin prickled with a familiar agitation.

"Reece, it's four-thirty in the morning. You don't have work, and Jessie does not need to be checked. She is sixteen years old. She'll wake up and eat breakfast whenever she needs to. She's got an exam later, but it's far too early for her to be awake. Just come back to bed, please." As she spoke, her voice remained calm but firm, and her eyes searched mine. I recalled a hint of anxiety in her face.

"It's not four thirty. Don't be ridiculous. It's just after seven. I've got to be at work soon, and you're going to make me late. Why don't you just fucking listen?"

She flinched then, like I had slapped her across the cheek. My words had hurt her. I could see, but it was unexplainable and volcanic. And just as soon as the feeling had come, it expired again. Lois gave her head a sharp shake in response. For the first time, I noticed the patches of grey in her hair, behind her ears, on the crown of her head. Odd, I hadn't noticed them yesterday.

"I'm not going to argue with you, Reece. Take a look outside and tell me why it's still dark when it's just after seven a.m. in the middle of May." Lois marched over to the window and yanked the blind upwards.

My heart sank. She was right; the sky was mostly dark, but there was a pink hue that only appeared in the smallest hours of the morning. For the first time that day, I sneaked a sidelong look at the time on the digital display on the oven: 4:28 a.m. Ah.

"Now please, just go back to bed. This isn't you talking." She put her head in her hands, and by the red blotching of her skin, I could tell she was trying not to cry.

In that moment, it felt as if I had just been given my first breath after being deprived of oxygen. Like I had been dragged under water for miles and then allowed to resurface. My mind cleared in an instant.

She was right; this wasn't me. It was my body, my words, and my actions. It was my decision to wake up and come downstairs so early that morning. But…it also wasn't. Something else played a part in my choices now. There seemed to be a third party looming in the back of my mind, tearing out chunks of grey matter and playing tricks on me. A civil war raged inside my mind, and I wasn't even sure when it started or whose side I was meant to be on. And the worst thing, I kept forgetting that the fucker was there, and all the while its grip was getting tighter and tighter.

My brain stumbled over its own awkwardly placed hurdles, loping uneasily over them until the words I needed came to me. A question forced itself to the front of my mind.

"What year is it?" I asked tentatively, all my earlier confidence gone.

I felt small and insecure, and most of all I felt wrong. I felt like I was watching a version of myself from behind a huge wall of glass. And I was banging on that glass, trying to get the other me to listen and to cooperate, but this huge partition stifled any noise I made.

"What year do you *think* it is?" Lois shot back. Her head did not move from her hands. She rocked forward slowly, waiting for an answer.

"Is it 2018?" I guessed. I knew as soon as it left my mouth that it was wrong, even though moments ago I had been so sure.

How fragile reality is; until Lois had found me in the kitchen, I had been so sure of everything. And now it had all been thrown into doubt. And for all I knew, whatever information I was being fed could have been just as false too. That was the most worrying part. In a world where you believed everything you were told, who could you trust?

"It's 2031, Reece. We have been married twenty-one years, we have one daughter, she is sixteen years old, and her name is Jessie. She's in her last year of school." Lois paused before the next part of her speech. "You're sick, and you have been for a long time."

She looked up from her hands, and I found myself nodding as the truth of her words settled upon me. My heart felt heavy because somehow I knew that this wasn't the first time I had heard this, and yet I knew it would not be the last time, either.

These facts must have been predetermined. The facts were instructions; they were there to bring me back to the present and back to reality.

"I'm sorry," I mumbled. I sounded like a scorned child, and that was what I felt like. I could practically feel my bottom lip beginning to pout. *It's the Alzheimer's,* I wanted to say. Surely I should be pitied rather than scolded? Surely I should be forgiven? Surely Lois should have been more patient?

Surely she knew that this disease was so unforgiving in its assault that it would never give me peace. It was relentless. It didn't have favourites; it didn't have a conscience, and it was not prejudiced. When it came to my memories, it would crush them with a Godzilla-like finesse. It would not wait for me to be ready. It would not let me rest. And there wasn't a single thing that I could do about it.

And in that moment, I hated myself. I truly did. I despised the disease that had not only taken my life from me but also had then made me forget what it had done, only to be reminded by somebody else. I knew that each time this happened, it had been preceded by a glimmer of hope; a moment in which my wife and I felt the illness might not make an appearance that day. Because that was what it did. On some days I woke up, and I was myself again; I made Lois breakfast, I helped Jessie with her revision, and then wham! It was all gone again. Snatched away in an instant.

I knew that I had broken my wife's heart many times before this moment, and yet I knew tomorrow that I would not be able to help myself, and I would do it all over again.

Tears spilled down my cheeks. I tried to cry silently. I didn't want to draw attention to myself, but my mouth betrayed me. It made an ugly U shape as I howled and sobbed uncontrollably. Crying was not a feeling that I was used to.

"It's OK. Hey, it's OK," Lois soothed. She was at my side in an instant, taking me into her arms. I had always been shorter than her, and I had always enjoyed being taken into her strong embrace. In that moment, it was no different. I nestled my face into the crook of her neck and tried to stop my tears.

I wished that the disease that plagued my brain would crawl back into the darkest and furthest corners of where it had come from. Would it ever retract all of its venom and allow the pathways of my mind to reopen so I could resume control of my life? It didn't seem likely, but as we stood in that kitchen together and my mind slowly reset itself, I wished for a cure, no matter how impossible it seemed.

Chapter 4

Two years earlier
October 2029

My back was to her, and I was bent over the sink, scrubbing hard at a grease-covered pan. Even without looking, I knew what she was doing. She was looking up at the ceiling, her lips drawn into a tight line. She was waiting for something...

"Reece, I think there's something wrong with you." The words tumbled out all at once. Like a river that had finally burst its banks, I knew that they had been building up for a long time before this moment.

And here they were. They had been tossed out into the kitchen, and no matter how well planned, they felt careless to me, those words. They rattled around, rebounded off the overhead cupboards, and shook the walls on impact. It was a small statement, but its magnitude was similar to that of a highly explosive volcano.

But the worst thing was that she was right. The thoughts that she had just expressed were not hers alone; I had suspected it for some time too. It had gone on for so long it had begun to be a heavy cloud over our relationship, and it had been threatening to erupt and shower us both at any moment. I could see that now.

Now that the words were out there, neither of us could decide what to do with them. For a while, we beat those words around like we were playing a game of tennis. Both of us were unwilling to take the lion's share of the responsibility. Lois wished they had never been spoken, that she hadn't even opened her mouth, and I wished that I had never heard them. Both of us wished that we had simply followed Jessie upstairs and that the three of us had swept the matter under the carpet to be forgotten about for another week.

Until it inevitably happened again.

I had forgotten to collect Jessie from school; that was where this argument had stemmed from. She had waited four hours for somebody to come and collect her, and I had completely forgotten. I had finished work and come home and restlessly moved around the house, starting activities that I would abandon only moments later. But I had had this ridiculous, nagging feeling the whole time. The nagging feeling turned out to be a forgotten Jessie.

A forgotten Jessie who had turned up in the dark after walking the entire way home. A forgotten Jessie whose calls I had ignored because I had left my phone God knows where.

A heartbroken Jessie who had sobbed and sobbed in my arms when she finally arrived home, exhausted and scared.

And when Lois found out, she was absolutely furious. I couldn't recall another time when she had been so angry with me. She had sent Jessie to her room and then spent the next half hour screaming at me that I was irresponsible and selfish until finally we had reached this moment. My back to her, my hands in the sink. At her words, I had dropped the pan back into the soapy water.

I had a hard time acknowledging the truth to her words. Now somebody else had noticed my peculiar actions—the forgetfulness, the irrational mood swings, the sudden fits of rummaging through drawers and cupboards in a bid to find something that I soon forgot the name of or sometimes forgot what I was looking for entirely. While it had been rattling around in my mind, unbeknownst to me it had been adding up in Lois's too.

"I know," I finally muttered, and I heard Lois breathe a sigh of relief. Had she thought that I might not be so willing to agree with her? That was a possibility. When I was sick, I wasn't the easiest person to reason with. When I fell ill, I flat out denied it and felt a responsibility to be brave and soldier on no matter what. It was Lois who had to wrestle me back into bed and shove a cup of chicken soup under my nose.

"This isn't the first time you've forgotten something, and you know, I've forgiven you those other times because they haven't been so important. And I know you've been a little stressed out, so I've made allowances for that too. But to forget our own daughter?" Lois's voice rose as she spoke. "She is ever so upset. I can't let you do that to her again. This is getting to be too much of a problem for me to just ignore now. We need to take you to somebody. We need to get help for this."

As I let her speak, I found myself nodding in agreement. I was comforted by the fact that she was willing to share the weight. And I was comforted by how convincing she was. I had been thinking about going to the doctor for some time, but perhaps I needed to be *taken* there instead. I had hoped that I was still capable of going somewhere by myself but to have my wife's support would be invaluable.

"I know," I conceded, finally. Those two words again.

"I've already called the doctor. We're going this Thursday. I've moved some things around so that will be my next day off work and Jessie will be at her after-school club. I don't think we should tell her about this just yet. Let's get some answers first."

It was unsurprising to me that Lois had already called our doctor. She often announced carefully constructed plans that I had not even considered yet. Sometimes I supposed that came from her career in the police force.

What would happen to Lois's career? A fleeting thought that I pushed to the back of my mind. For this one moment in our relationship, I had to allow myself some time of my own. For once, I had to consider my own health and my own future before my wife's and my daughter's.

"Maybe it is just stress. You've not been sleeping well lately. They'll give you some antidepressants and a few sleeping pills. You could be back to normal in a few weeks, and we'll all be fine. We'll probably laugh about it in a few years. It's probably nothing." Lois chuckled to herself, but the sound was fake and her smile was unconvincing.

And in that moment, I knew that although Lois had gone through the hassle of arranging our days off work, had been in contact with our GP already, and had clearly been going over this scenario for months, she had still failed to acknowledge the reason behind all of my behaviour. She hadn't reached that far yet, hadn't been willing to make the calculations. My symptoms all added up to something that we were both fully conscious of, and yet we were too scared to admit it to ourselves and to each other.

If we spoke those dreaded words out loud, then that would be a step too far.

I didn't need to see a doctor for a diagnosis; I knew with despairing confidence what I had. There was enough about it in the news for me to glean all the information I needed to self-diagnose pretty efficiently. I didn't need somebody to tell me something I already knew.

The real reason we had to go to that doctor and I had to partake in the various humiliating tests that now seemed inevitable was so Lois could finally accept it. Lois needed to hear it from somebody else; she needed the validation of a professional for her to admit that what I had was not just due to stress. What did I even have to be stressed about?

Worst of all, we needed a doctor to tell us the problem. Lois was not one to trust hearsay or gossip. She needed facts and lots of them. That was what made her plans so foolproof. In this case, the doctor held those facts. It was our doctor alone who could either make or break Lois. And if I were honest, I thought it was the latter. Lois was strong, but she wasn't invincible.

I pulled my hands out of the water and peeled off the rubber gloves I had been wearing.

What will happen to my career? I thought. *Will I be able to continue teaching?*

Probably not. It wouldn't be safe. It wouldn't be satisfactory, either. Parents would notice, and those students who still gave a fuck about learning would become upset about the lack of consistency that I would bring to my teaching. I was convinced that even now my teaching ability was on the brink of absolute collapse before this thing inside my brain had even really got started.

I would have to give it all up, after qualifying barely two decades ago. My dreams would be put on hold indefinitely. It all depended upon if I would be well enough to come back. If it was a brain tumour, which it looked like it could be, then I could die. It could be inoperable. My best-case scenario might be that I had to take a year out to recover.

My aspirations of becoming a head teacher and the possibility of completing a doctorate degree were shrinking at an astronomical rate.

To my intense shame, I began to cry. For months, I had pushed these thoughts to the back of my mind. I knew that if I had given them a second of the airtime that they so desperately desired, then I wouldn't be able to cope with where they took me. I had identified the thoughts as parasitic, and they weren't to have a place in my mind. But they were there. Oh, they were there, and they had been all along. They weren't going anywhere, they told me. They had only just begun.

Since my back was to her, my tears went unnoticed by Lois; neither of us spoke. What was there to say? What was to become of our future together? In that moment, with more questions than answers to match, it was far too terrifying to bear thinking about.

We each allowed the other to reflect upon the conversation we had just had, and I prayed that my tears would continue to go unnoticed to allow Lois the space she required.

I realised with some irony that the scene itself seemed to be a magnification of our entire marriage. I was drowning in the freezing depths of the ocean as Lois stood at the shoreline with her back to the sea. With each wave that threatened to drag me under the surf, I remained quiet, patient and waiting. I would not allow my own panic to take over. Instead, I allowed Lois a little more time to engage with her own feelings, as I always did. After all, it wouldn't be long before Lois would have to brave the depths herself.

🙏

Doctor Thomas had thick, wild grey hair and glasses that rested on the top of her large, high forehead, supported by a heavyset brow. She wore jeans and a loose button-down shirt, I noticed. The casual choice of clothing was a bid to make her patients feel more relaxed, the result of a recent study. However, doctors appeared to be increasingly eccentric over their clothing choices now than they had been when I was growing up. I had once taken a nine-year-old Jessie to see a doctor who wore jeans and a battered T-shirt with characters from *The Simpsons*, which had been cancelled eight years earlier.

It had been two months since Lois had confronted me in the kitchen after I had forgotten to collect Jessie from school. Since then, I had gone through several tests, some of which seemed completely irrelevant and appeared to be so easy that I barely saw the benefit. As time passed and I answered the similar questions each week, I slowly crept out of my confident state of denial. With each day that passed, I was becoming more and more aware of the fact that my mind was deteriorating. Now it seemed even more obvious to me that my mind was in a dangerous free fall. And it was positively terrifying.

What made it worse was the waiting. It felt like the doctors were allowing this thing to make as much damage as it could while it still had time.

On some days, I wished that these appointments would come sooner so whatever was in my head could be taken out and I could resume my life. But on other days, I dreaded them. I wished that they would never come because it meant facing the truth of my situation. I might have cancer. I might have to go through chemo or have half of my brain removed or who knew what else? And two months seemed like an excruciatingly long time to wait for the conclusion to my story.

I didn't know which was worse, the possibility of being aware of my slow descent into madness or the prospect of being so far gone that my brain activity no longer gave me lucidity over the situation. Perhaps it would be a relief to have declined so much that I could no longer tell anything was wrong with me. How lovely it would be to skip the entire decline and go straight to the part where I was bedbound and didn't have a clue who I was or where I was, and I didn't care, either. Or not to have it at all.

Between visits to the doctor and the neurologist, my overall condition seemed to yo-yo. On some days, I felt perfectly normal and almost considered the possibility of cancelling all further appointments. On other days, I lost things, I stumbled over my sentences, and at my worst I forgot where I was. These days were particularly frightening and allowed a dark depression at the prospect of where my mind might end up should I not receive any treatment to envelop me.

"Well, Reece, Lois." Doctor Thomas nodded at each of us in turn. "Thanks for coming in today, and thank you for taking the time to go to all of the appointments that we scheduled for you. I know it's been incredibly stressful for you both." She paused. And when a doctor pauses, you know nothing good will ever follow. "We have received the results from the neurologist, and I'm afraid it isn't good news…"

Next to me, I heard Lois's breath catch in her throat; her chest had stopped moving beneath her shirt. I maintained my own steady breathing for the both of us. I was determined to remain calm. This was not the end. This could not be the end. But if it was, then one of us had to stay strong.

"Throughout the tests, the neurologist noticed an extreme cognitive decline. Your cognitive function, including your short-term memory, confirmed our suspicions that you are in the first stage of early-onset Alzheimer's disease."

It was my turn for my breath to catch in my throat. A freight train had smashed into my chest.

I had thought…I had thought I had a tumour. I had thought I might have some chemo, that I might have an operation and the tumour would be removed or reduced. Almost all kinds of tumours, wherever they cropped up, were operable now. You had a high chance of surviving anything cancer threw at you. But this—Alzheimer's—it was much worse.

I broke away from my body then; I couldn't listen anymore. My mind had gone elsewhere. It floated above my body, dancing around like a child, humming under its breath, fingers in its ears. "La la la, I can't hear you," I imagined it singing to the doctor. Was there much point in listening to what was said now? The diagnosis was enough. It was practically a death sentence.

"What can we do?" I heard Lois ask from somewhere at my side. The question made me realise that this is what it would be like for future appointments; my participation would no longer be required. My responses would no longer be valid nor relied upon to be truthful. I would be ignored in favour of my wife's experiences. My wife's opinion would far outweigh my own.

I may as well sign my life over right now, I resolved. Because that's what you had to do when you got Alzheimer's. You gave your life to somebody you trusted—your partner, your children—and you said goodnight, you said your prayers, you got your affairs in order while you still could, and that was that.

But I wasn't ready to say goodnight. I wasn't even fifty years old. I wasn't even what you could call middle-aged.

"As I said, Reece is in the first stages of the disease. We've caught it quite early on, so you will have a lot of time to prepare and adjust to the lifestyle that Reece will soon have to follow. There's no telling how quickly she will deteriorate." The doctor waited.

Lois was shutting down. Her eyes had begun to glaze over, and her coping mechanisms were clicking into place.

"One day you might notice that she will start forgetting important life events. She may even fail to recognise you or your daughter. And when these things happen, it is very important that you are patient with her. Some days will be better than others, but it's also vital that you remember she may never again be able to recall the memories that are lost. It's up to you to remind her of them, but don't be frustrated when she cannot enjoy the same sense of nostalgia that you had once shared."

It wasn't cancer. It wasn't cancer.

I turned to Lois, my face contorted in confusion, in desperation. I wished that she would look at me, hold my hand, rub my arm, anything to make me feel like I wasn't completely alone.

"A lot of patients and their families formulate a predetermined set of facts that they repeat to the patient in times when their memories are particularly bad. Instead of being frustrated with Reece, each time she forgets a familiar face or has lost the link that ties you to her, the family member should state these facts clearly.

"For example, remind Reece that she was once a teacher. Tell her how long you have been married...those sorts of things. I've supplied you with a list of helpful websites. There are various articles that you can download and read that will be useful to you.

"But, Lois and Reece, you must both understand that sufficient plans for the future must be made whilst you are still able to. You'll need to get in touch with your lawyer, make financial arrangements, those sorts of things. And I know you won't want to consider this yet, but you have to think about the possibility of putting Reece into a home at some point too…"

⁂

Lois drove us home in utter silence. She had not spoken a word since we left the doctor's office. At the time, and after her initial fuzzy-headed state, she had been full of questions. Questions that I had barely heard through the heavy fog that had settled on my own shocked brain. Words like "how" and "long" and "why" floating through here and there. I was grateful that Lois had been there to ask the questions and absorb the information. And it occurred to me that it didn't really matter whether I heard any of the doctor's words. Why would it matter to me in the months and years that followed? I wouldn't even be here.

Perhaps it would be quick. Maybe one week I would forget to collect my daughter from school and then the next I would forget how to use the toilet and then the week after that I would be dead. Quickly succumbing to pneumonia or some blood infection or other.

I hoped that however I died, it would be quick for my family's sake. I hoped that I would die without fuss. That I would die gently in my sleep after a sufficient time of suffering had passed and I had time to settle my affairs and say goodbye. Perhaps that was something I had always rooted for. I was aware that throughout life, when human beings questioned their own mortality, there was always a perverse hope that death would be quick or painless, and if you were lucky, it would be both.

My thoughts wandered to Jessie, so young, so full of life. What about her? She shared my DNA. The good DNA and now the horrifically bad DNA too. Would it be possible to find out if Jessie was safe from the disease? There were tests that she could take. But maybe she wouldn't want to know, especially if there was little she could do about it anyway.

A pain gathered in my chest at the thought of her inheriting this disease. It was bad enough to have it myself, but to be to blame for giving it to my one and only child—that was truly devastating. Would Jessie begin to abhor me just as much as I abhorred my own biological mother and father?

⭑

Lois swung the car into the driveway. The front and side parking sensors let out a dull beep, and she switched the engine off. She didn't move; she only stared straight ahead at the brickwork of our house.

Our gorgeous home: red brick, two floors, beautiful garden, driveway—that's what the advert had said. "Needs some modernisation," it had described. The estate agent had suggested a low offer and it would be ours in a few weeks if we were willing to put the work in and renovate it. Newly married, we had snapped it up. It was our dream home, and after moving in, we had set about making the necessary arrangements. Both surreptitiously hinting to each other that the second bedroom could be a nursery one day.

See? I remembered all of that, every single detail of moving into our new home. I felt like I could recall every single ugly item that had covered the floor space of our home throughout the years. But why was it that I could remember these things but I couldn't remember my own daughter's name at times? That was what I hated most, that I could remember such trivial things that had no bearing on my life but for some absurd reason my mind chose to throw away those important memories that were catastrophic if forgotten.

There were also the more precious memories. Jessie's first day at school. Her first steps. Where had they gone? I had been there for all of them. I wouldn't have missed a second of my daughter's childhood, and yet the memories had vanished. In their place was a dark haziness that seemed to engulf my mind one memory at a time. And there hadn't even been a warning that they would soon disappear; I hadn't even had time to write them down.

If I tried hard enough, I thought I could picture these things, but was I just making it up? Were they really memories of my daughter? Or could they just be something I conjured up to reassure myself that the disease wasn't already taking everything I had ever loved?

Disease. It didn't sound right to me. A disease was something that you could see; it stretched over the skin, made you throw up, gave you headaches, and stole your hair. It made me feel like an imposter, the idea that I was sick but that there was nothing on the outside to tell people so.

The doctor had prescribed me with a vast cocktail of medication, including those antidepressants Lois had been so hopeful for, like she thought those would solve all our problems. There was a thing called Tanzepitzil too. I had been instructed to start taking this particular drug straight away in a bid to slow the symptoms I was experiencing.

Would it work? Lois had demanded. *Could these drugs save Reece?*

The doctor had made a noncommittal shrug and said, "There are some rumours that Medipharm Inc. is working on something. But it's years from completion. At the moment, there is no cure." It had reaffirmed our fears. I would never be rid of the disease entirely, would never be free from how my brain was slowly rotting away. I could only put up a good fight until it inevitably took over completely.

And that was that.

No cure.

It was a death sentence. Thrust into our hands without any sign of an apology. The doctor went on to her next patient seamlessly and without any disruption to her conscience. But who was there to blame? Not her. Not my foster families. I knew that what I had was genetic. It was not something my adoptive family could have foreseen or prevented.

Was it fair to blame my biological parents? At the time, when I was looking for somebody, anybody, to be at fault, I had silently raged at my biological parents and how careless they had been when they passed on this defective gene to their daughter. Perhaps if I had agreed to meet my biological mother, then I might have discovered my fate earlier. Not that there was anything I could have done about it even then; there were no effective preventive measures for what my DNA had planned for me. And for Jessie.

"What do we do now?" I asked, finally breaking our silence.

Lois would have a plan. Lois always had a plan ready and waiting in the wings. She had probably been conceiving something the entire ride home.

But "I don't know" were all the words she could muster before she began to sob.

⋏

I lay awake that night and considered my own fate and how much more of my life I possibly had to live.

I randomly stabbed at memories from Lois's and my past and begged my mind to keep them. To store them and safeguard them away from the prying eyes of my disease. I tested myself with these memories, imagined the clothing I had worn in them, the feelings I had felt, the words I had said. And I wished more than anything that these thoughts would be the very last things to leave me.

CHAPTER 5

Twenty-two years earlier
February 2007

My original plans for the day were meant to be: revise, study, revise, write, revise, and drink coffee…and so on. The first year of my English degree had been going pretty well so far, and I couldn't bear the idea of failing my exams by the time they came around, so I started the revision a lot earlier than most.

An hour or so after I had finally dragged myself out of bed, I stumbled through the door of my local café. A place I often found myself using as a spot to be constructive with my university work. When I arrived, I dumped my things into the seat of one of the high-backed chairs that framed a table in the corner of the café. I ordered a coffee.

The assistant rang my order through the till and called to his colleague to start making my drink. He had a face that made him look as if he were perpetually pissed off—a face that my mother would have described as a "bulldog chewing a wasp."

Now, I was never a believer in love at first sight. There is lust at first sight, sure. But not love. I still don't think there's such thing as love at first sight, but as I looked over his shoulder and I saw her for the very first time—well, I'm fairly sure that came pretty close to it. As soon as my eyes met hers, my heart started to pound so hard that it felt like it might burst out of my chest or make a flying leap out of my mouth. In return, all she gave me was a sly smirk. Like she could read my thoughts.

The assistant in front of me flicked his hand in the direction of the next counter, instructing me to move on. I realised then that I had been staring at this girl, and my face flushed. My only consolation was that she had been looking at me too, with that damn arrogant smile playing on her lips.

She turned her back to me, added the final touches to my drink, and placed it on the counter in front of me. Giving me the smallest wink, she turned back to the coffee machine. That auburn hair that I would come to know and adore was tied up in a ponytail. It flicked around her shoulders as she worked furiously to make the next batch of coffees. My eyes were out on stalks, the shape of them transformed into hearts, like the way cartoon characters go when they spot something they like.

I shuffled over to my table, careful not to spill my coffee. As I made my journey, I cursed myself for not saying something witty. I knew right then that I would have done anything to see that girl's smile.

As I worked, I contemplated the idea of asking the girl out for a drink when she got off work. Initially, the thought sent me into a swirling vortex of panic, and I almost pushed the idea straight to the back of my mind, discarded. I had never asked a girl out before. It was an act that was far beyond my remit, and I was getting ahead of myself. *But…it couldn't hurt, could it?* I reasoned. I mean really, what did I have to lose?

At two minutes past five, armed with an uncharacteristic confidence—possibly due to the vast amount of coffee I had consumed because I had revisited the counter a further six times just so I could see her again—I began to rise from my seat.

But I was too late. I caught a glimpse of that bright auburn hair as she shut the café door behind her and linked arms with a man, soon out of sight. Ah, of course. I couldn't believe I hadn't realised it before. How easily I had fallen in love in the space of a few hours. It was tragic really.

Initially, the caffeine numbed my thoughts, but I couldn't stop the disappointment from enveloping me entirely. It flooded my body, reaching all the way to the tips of my fingers and toes. *It wasn't meant to be,* I tried to repeat to myself as I packed up my things.

⋏

A few months later, I lay in bed. The girl next to me stared up at the ceiling and examined the cracks that snaked across its surface. Weird shadows appeared on the walls, made from the movement of her hands in the light of my bedside lamp. Her auburn hair spilled across the pillow that we were sharing in my cramped single bed.

It was 3:00 a.m.; later that day, I would return to my family after my first year at university.

"I've had an idea," she said. As she finally spoke, it dawned on me that she had been fairly quiet all evening, something that I wasn't used to when in her company.

"Yeah, what's that?" I was looking at her now. I admired her profile, her strong jawline, the curve of her nose, and the freckles on her cheeks.

"You should just stay here all summer," she suggested. She held up her hands and examined them in the same way she had just looked at the ceiling. It was a tactic that tried to display a lack of interest in her conversation. It was a similar act of flippancy that she always tried to employ when we discussed vaguely serious matters back then.

My pulse roared in my ears and tried to steady the drumming of my heart. I was so sure that she would hear it.

"We could hang out, you know, see some films. Go to the park. Stay in bed…that kinda thing," the girl continued coolly.

She still didn't look in my direction; instead, her eyes were fixed upon the strand of red hair that she was now playing with. Twisting it around and around her index finger and then letting it go, a curl forming.

"But my family are waiting for me…" I started halfheartedly. She heard it in my voice then, my uncertainty, my willingness to be led wherever she wanted to take me.

I had seen her again, after that time in the café. I ran into her at a student party a few weeks afterwards. Initially, I spent the evening trying to avoid her, trying to disengage from any contact. I wouldn't meet her eyes across the room, though I knew she was watching me. I would leave areas within seconds of her entering and hide myself away in the bathroom until I knew she was no longer looking for me.

Until she caught me, of course.

"Hey, you!" she had practically shouted in my ear. She caught me off guard whilst I poured myself a drink, causing me to spill it all over my hands. "Are you gonna stop tryna hide from me?" She snatched the bottle of lemonade from me and drank from it. As I listened to her, I noted her Yorkshire accent. It was soft. But it was undeniable, and it rolled from her mouth like the notes of a symphony. It was more pronounced on certain words; instead of "you" she said "yer," and she contracted certain words until they almost made up a new language.

"I'm not—I'm not trying to hide from you," I stuttered.

"Funny that, because you seem to keep leaving the room (*t'room*) every time I come in. And you've hidden in't bathroom (*baa-throom*) at least twice tonight just to avoid me."

"You're pretty arrogant, aren't you?" I said before I could stop myself. My face flushed, but she burst out laughing.

"I'm right though, aren't I?"

"You might be," I replied. I finally met her gaze, and my knees shook beneath me.

"I'm Lois. What's your name?"

"Reece."

"Ah, Reece, so do you want to get out of here or what?"

And just like that, there was no way that I could have refused her. She was enchanting and charming and enigmatic all at the same time, and I couldn't resist. She gave me that look, that look that she would give me for years to come. Piercing, knowing. A look that said everything I needed to hear.

And so there we were, in bed together. My hand close enough to touch hers but still not daring to. My heart thudding in my ears. We had found ourselves in a stalemate; each waited for the other to say the first thing. Lois appeared to be overcome with an uncharacteristic shyness, and I continued to feel just as painfully awkward as I always had.

Sometimes I think back on it and imagine that morning when we lay in bed together. I guess it seemed like an easy decision at the time, me staying with her for the summer. But what would have happened had I gone home? Home was a few hours away in the car. Would we have been willing to travel all that way to see each other, having only known each other for a few months?

Something told me that Lois would have been willing. She seemed to be pushy and persistent with everything she did. And I think she prided herself on that ability, and I allowed myself to be nudged into things.

"I suppose I could," I finally agreed. I suppose I added up everything that had happened since before we met. Me choosing her café out of the hundreds in our city, me missing the opportunity to ask her out but then finding her at the party not long after, her persistence at that party despite my best efforts to avoid her…it all seemed to add up to something. Whatever I did, Lois just seemed to be inevitable to me.

Chapter 6

Twenty-five years later
January 2032

I awoke early. It was the second day of the new year, and I wasn't usually one for setting resolutions, but I vowed to return to the more promising and positive roots of my youth. Realistically, Reece wasn't going to get better, and I knew that. It had taken me a stupidly long time to accept it, but I had now.

Before, when she had first been diagnosed, I had been helplessly in denial. It was either denial or a false sense of hopefulness. No matter how much the odds are stacked up against you, when somebody you love is diagnosed with a terminal illness, every single unrealistic part of you hopes that she will be her own miracle, an exception to the rule. My feelings about Reece's mortality were no different.

Until now.

There was movement beside me, and I felt an eruption of guilt-induced butterflies in my abdomen. I counted to ten in my head and turned over. I locked eyes with Reece's.

Her hazel eyes were swimming with tears, the redness of them highlighted the green flecks in her irises. The sight of them made my stomach lurch again, but I pushed the feeling away. I mentally scanned through all of the possible scenarios and reasons that might have led up to this moment. That's how it was now. Every morning I woke to some problem, some horrible scenario that Reece had found herself in.

As the rest of my body caught up with my mind, I realised that the bed sheets I rested on were damp. She had wet herself again. I held my body still so that the wave of revulsion I felt would go unnoticed by her. I visualised changing the bed sheets yet again and let out a sigh.

"I'm sorry," Reece whimpered. Her bottom lip quivered with impending sobs.

"Hey, it's OK," I muttered. "Come on, we'll get this sorted out." I climbed reluctantly out of bed and helped her into a chair in the corner of the room. I allowed myself a small, selfish thought before I began. Oh God, how badly I wanted this to be over.

I stripped the bed as she watched me from her position. When the bed was bare, I carried the soiled sheets, one of which was a plastic mattress protector, and dumped them all in the laundry basket. I had recently considered the possibility of getting Reece to wear nappies, but the thought had been too much to bear. Had Reece been fully mentally competent, she would have refused the idea straight away too. It was just one more humiliating experience to add to the ever-growing list of things neither of us felt ready for. But it would have been enormously helpful had she agreed to it.

I layered a new protective sheet under the fitted sheet and ensured that the corners were secure and wouldn't pull up in the night. In the absence of adult nappies, I had purchased several of these helpful reusable protective sheets, and they had been invaluable in previous months.

Reece watched as I made up a new duvet and pillows. I had done this so often recently that I was becoming quite an expert. Though my mind often drifted longingly to those nappies again. Nappies would mean less mess…

Next, I slowly pulled Reece into a clean pair of pyjamas, guiding her emaciated limbs through their respective holes. I lowered her back in the bed and tucked the sheets right up to her neck.

"I'm sorry," she murmured again as I knelt beside the bed. "I couldn't help it."

"It's OK," I soothed. I stroked a loose curl away from her forehead. A gesture that, years ago, would have felt tender and loving. Now it just felt like a forced routine. I looked past her searching eyes and onto the table next to the bed. A cache of pills piled up on the side. A stack of books, all gathering dust.

I couldn't wait for it to all be gone.

"D-do you still love me?" Reece asked. My eyes flicked over her earnest expression, and it made my stomach drop.

She had noticed something; she must have.

I forced myself to make eye contact with her again, to look into those hazel eyes, still red and full with tears. Tears of humiliation and desperation. I realised that she was waiting for validation still. But I wasn't sure if I could give it.

Here was this woman, this woman who I was meant to love in sickness and in health, and I didn't know if I could anymore. Or if I even still did. Of course I loved *my* Reece. I adored the woman she once was.

Back when she was healthy, she had often told me that I was cold and too detached, but I was capable of love, and I did love her. Still did. I still did love her. I loved her so much it hurt, but at that moment, I was having a hard time trying to find that love. The kind of love that she wanted and needed.

I gulped back a cluster of tears that had gathered in the back of my throat.

"Of course I do, of course. Just go back to sleep for a bit. I'm going to shower, OK?" I gave her hands a light squeeze and kissed her on the forehead as I stood.

Yes, I loved her. If I didn't love her, then I wouldn't still be here. At least, that's what I kept telling myself.

I walked over to our shared wardrobe and pulled out a pair of jeans, some underwear, socks, and a clean white T-shirt; I laid them on the bed for Reece to change into when she was out of bed again. I tried to anticipate the order in which she might put her clothes on, but with her illness, I could predict very little now. For myself, I pulled out my own pair of black jeans and a navy blue jumper. I carried my clothing to the bathroom and draped them over the counter to change into after I had finished showering.

I shut the bathroom door and prayed that I wouldn't be disturbed for twenty minutes. That's all I wanted, just twenty minutes to myself in the morning, and then I felt like I could get through the day.

When I finished my shower, I gently patted myself dry and mentally listed the things I would need to do today. Really, I should have been back at work at least two days ago to help the force with the epidemic of drunks on New Year's Eve; however, my boss had granted me with an entire two weeks' leave over the holiday period.

His undeserved amount of pity was beginning to get embarrassing.

It was worse for Jessie, though, the pity. People were horrified to learn that she was the daughter of an Alzheimer's sufferer. "Your mother is so young!" they would claim. "I'm so sorry to hear that." And then finally, their favourite phrase: "There's no cure for that, is there?"

"There's no cure." I couldn't count the number of times I had heard that. As if I needed reminding about our hopeless situation.

Friends who claimed that they would stick around never did. They were gone as soon as Reece's symptoms had started to become more noticeable. Her work colleagues had sent her bunches of flowers and a card that they had all signed. They had even taken her out for dinner for what they had delicately described as her "early retirement," and then that was it. They had disappeared completely.

My own friends politely refused to come to the house when invited now too, and I could hardly blame them. Who wanted to sit in the same room as somebody with Alzheimer's? It was like staring into your own desolate future. And my spare time was so consumed by caring for Reece that I was unable to entertain guests anyway.

I could understand people staying away because of their fear of Reece and her condition, but I was still here. Those people had been my friends too, and they owed me enough to stick around and be a suitable support network. I would have done it for them. But in the years since Reece's diagnosis, I found that other than the initial, "You poor thing having to take care of her. It must be awful for you," people rarely cared about me. And it was disappointing to me that my own boss cared more about me than my friends.

On the whole, the concern always revolved around Reece and her general health and well-being. People seemed to forget that I had feelings too. No, I wasn't unwell, and no, Reece had not died, but I still had to take care of her. Still had to dedicate all of my free time to tend to her needs. Still had to watch my partner suffer. Was I not allowed to feel sadness or anger or bitterness? Were those feelings reserved only for the sick and the dying?

And I was sad, I was angry, I was bitter. It was that bitterness that had pulled me away from Reece, and I hadn't been conscious of it until it was too late. I still loved her somehow.

In some deep, discarded part of me, I adored her, but I just couldn't reach that part at the moment, no matter how hard I tried. God, how much did I wish that it hadn't ended like this?

I blow-dried my hair quickly and tied it in a loose bun on top of my head. I hadn't put any clothes on yet so I took the spare time I had by myself to admire my figure in the mirror. At forty-eight years old, I still felt confident about my body, still felt physically able to conduct my job above the expected standard, and could still outrun even the fastest criminals. Although it had long ago started to sag in some places and I had picked up a few scars along the way, a minor hazard of the job, I could still say that I loved the body that looked back at me in the mirror.

I had always thought it was vital to love yourself, even on the bad days when you felt like you weren't deserving enough of love. On those days, it was especially important. I had always hoped that by living my life carefully abiding by this attitude, my daughter would follow my mindset and be just as happy in herself too.

I ran my finger over the long, inch-thick white scar that gouged a valley on the landscape of my thigh. A robbery gone wrong, I recalled. I pushed down lightly on the circular bullet-shaped wound on my left shoulder blade, a drugs raid gone awry. Each scar on my body was a lesson learnt. When I had been younger and still a teen, I might have attempted to hide these scars, but now I wore them proudly. They showed the world all of the second chances I had been given.

OK, so the injuries weren't life threatening per se, but they could have been. And for a second, when the blood is pouring out of a laceration to your arm or a deep gash in your leg, you believe that you will die, right there and then. Those occasions when I lay on the ground, holding tightly to my new wounds, I had started to think of all the things that I would miss and think of all the people who would miss me when I was no longer around.

It was inevitable really, when you were in my line of work, that something could go wrong. It didn't matter how far in advance you planned things; people were still unpredictable. Maybe that was what had drawn me to the job initially. In my carefully primed and preened world, I needed that instability. But I had two things to rock the boat now, my job *and* my wife. Reece was far less predictable than my job, though, and from time to time, her volatile moods were too much to bear.

Sometimes when my work partner and I cruised around in our police car, I hoped that that particular day might be my last one on the beat. A morbid thought that had to be ignored, but I found it making an appearance more and more often. Funny how the human brain works; it can't face what it must or it can't find a logical escape route, so it decides the next best option is death.

In these moments, I had to remind myself that I could never abandon my daughter, and I would force myself to consider the more rational methods of escape. A care home for Reece was one. Divorce or separation was another. On a more drastic level, there was murder, of course, or assisted suicide. Somebody might have thought that I was acting coldly, that I didn't care for Reece enough, but assisted suicide was something we had actually considered at a point when Reece was still coherent.

In the early days, she had brought it up more and more often. "I want to go quickly. It's not fair on you to drag this out any longer than it needs to," was her general line of argument. I had objected without hesitation; to agree to it would have gone against all of my basic instincts, and I couldn't believe she expected me to stand there and promise to help the woman I loved kill herself. And yet when Reece's gradual decline took a sudden, sharper fall, the idea resurfaced in my mind.

It had been too late by then, of course; Reece couldn't recall our old conversations, and she lacked the mental capacity to be talked into it by me. The window of opportunity to make that decision and follow it through had slammed shut. And no matter how much I threw my fists at its glass panes, it would never open again.

Staying, that was my chosen option. That was what I had decided, and that was what I must do. I couldn't live with myself if I just packed up and left. Not that she would ever have noticed. Out of sight, out of mind. And that's what I couldn't bear. I couldn't bear that one day she wouldn't even be able to call me by my own name. That's why I had come to feel the way that I did. My heart and my head were both trying to shut down any feelings I had for Reece in a bid to protect themselves in the long run. My mind right now was a therapist's dream, a great big, tangled web of guilt, denial, and avoidance.

I had to stay.

But all the while I considered this unknown stretch of our marriage in front of me, I almost envied those people who had decided to leave at the very beginning. I had read about it often online; the woman is diagnosed with breast cancer, and the next week her partner disappears into the ether. It was an awful thing to be jealous of, and I reprimanded myself each time these thoughts crept up on me. Those kinds of people were meant to be frowned upon for their cowardice, not praised.

Now it was all a waiting game. With every day that passed, Reece became more ill, her mind more and more fragmented as the weeks went on. On our worst days, when Reece was irritable, uncooperative, and completely cruel, I secretly prayed for her death. And it would have been a huge relief to have her finally pass away peacefully; I won't deny that. It would have unburdened both Jessie and me to not have to plan our lives around Reece anymore. And I was sure that Reece would have agreed had she still been able to make that decision.

Each time I had these hideous fantasies about Reece's death, I was always overcome with crippling guilt. Afterwards, to satisfy my own conscience, I would spend all day trying to entertain her and her two-second memory span.

I took one final look at my body in the mirror and began to put my clothes on now that I had dried off. I hung my damp towel on the heated rack in the bathroom and allowed the light to switch itself off as I left.

When I entered the bedroom next door, I saw Reece was no longer in bed. She was standing up and looking at the room around her. She was trying to figure out where she was, I guessed. That happened quite a lot then; when Reece wasn't confused about who she was, she was concerned about where she was.

She turned her face towards me. A deep gorge ran down her forehead as she absorbed the view. Her expression darkened by the second.

This was something new entirely, and my heart sunk. Normally, even when Reece was struggling with her orientation, as soon as she saw me, her eyes would light up in recognition and her face would split into a smile. This time, that frown was unchanging.

"Who are you? What are you doing in my house?" she asked quietly.

Panic began to rise in my throat. Tears that I had been keeping control of threatened to escape from my eyes.

She doesn't remember me. She thinks I'm just somebody who has broken into the house. I tried to step into her shoes. She was afraid, yes. And who wouldn't be afraid if they woke up and found a complete stranger was in their room? It was enough to terrify anyone, let alone somebody who was easily confused already.

But this was it. This was the beginning of the end. And despite the fact that my heart had begun to shut itself away from my feelings for Reece, I felt crushed. The cracks that had already formed on the surface of my heart slowly deepened into valleys, and an entire earthquake shattered my chest.

"I'm Lois," I replied, that earthquake shaking my voice as my words left my mouth. I had naively hoped that my name alone would be enough to pull her back to me. I had hoped that her mind would quickly but briefly rebuild the missing bridge between us and her face would split into a grin. That innocently happy smile she gave that made my chest pound with guilt.

Before this moment, I had hoped that our love was strong enough that Reece would never forget who I was. That I would never fall out of love with her. And now those hopes were completely crushed. How could somebody just forget the person she had spent almost her entire life with?

Yes, I knew that I had started to forget her too, but I had no other choice. It was either be forgotten or forget. But as much as I tried, I couldn't forget all of the moments I had shared with her. How could I? I was still stuck with them, no matter how hard I tried. Why was it so fucking easy yet so cruel for one person to forget these things, but I was not allowed to? I wanted there to be a pill I could take that would make me forget her too.

I wasn't allowed to panic. I was meant to be calm. I had to remember that this wasn't Reece who was talking. Somebody had gotten into her head and had torn out all of the connections, and no matter what she did to realign those wires, the thing inside her ripped out a few more each day.

"Who are you?" Reece's voice was slightly raised this time.

"It's me. It's Lois. I'm Lois, your wife." My voice wavered further. "Remember?" I added.

Please fucking remember me, I thought. *You can't have forgotten me already. It's too soon. I'm not ready. I'm not ready. I thought I was, but I'm not.*

Her face remained contorted into an ugly frown, and without thinking, I took a step towards her. I knew instantly that I had made a mistake, but it was too late. In response, she let out a deafening roar and gave me a violent shove. I fell backwards onto the chest of drawers behind me and pain shot up my back. I shouldn't have gone near her when she was so agitated. Jessie and I had learnt very early on that despite her frailty, she was able to throw a strong punch when she needed to. I had momentarily forgotten the rules we had laid out.

I recalled the moments when I had successfully subdued and disarmed a volatile situation with a criminal. Tried to choose the correct tone of voice to engage with the person in front of me. I wasn't even sure I could call this person my wife anymore; those days seemed to be fading fast with every second.

"I said, 'Who the fuck are you?'"

"I'm Lois. I am your wife. We have been married for twenty-two years. We have one child together, a daughter named Jessie. She is…" I was pleading by then. My voice was unsteady, and my words tumbled out in a mess. The calming methods forgotten, I begged for her to understand me. For the words to finally sink in. But that deep-set frown in her face would not waver. I had not convinced her yet. "I'm Lois. We met when you were at university. Please."

"I don't have a fucking daughter," Reece spat. "And I'm not married. If you keep lying to me, I'll just tell my counsellor, and they won't let me live with you anymore."

"W-what?"

"Don't be thick. You're her, aren't you? My new foster mother."

"I'm not—"

I stopped myself as it dawned on me that this was my chance. What had I read once before so long ago when Reece was first diagnosed? If the person you are caring for reaches the point where she no longer recognises you, then it is entirely useless for you to correct her. The article advised that you humour her, that you go along with everything she says. Allow her to live in the fantasy world she was in.

And I had noticed that Reece's chosen fantasy world was one from her younger years. In particular, the days when she was in the process of being fostered. It had been such an uncomfortable yet significant period in her life that her brain must have wanted to revisit it time and time again.

"Yes, I am," I found myself saying. "I've got the car outside. I've come to collect you. Make sure you've packed everything."

And as if I had spoken the magic words, Reece's face cleared, and she began to nod decisively to herself.

"I'll be downstairs in a minute. Just let me fucking pack my things."

Before she could add anything further to our exchange, I turned on my heel and left the room. I heard her let out a loud "tut" behind me, but I let it go. I was too relieved to say anything.

Once in the kitchen, I poured myself a mug of tea and took a seat at the large oak table. My tears subsided as I waited for Reece to join me. I hoped that this time we could restart the day in a better way than before.

Those butterflies were back again, and they swarmed in my stomach as I heard footsteps on the stairs and then in the hallway approaching the kitchen. Reece appeared at the door in the clothes that I had left for her; the T-shirt she wore was back to front, and the fly of her jeans remained unzipped below the button. I wasn't surprised to see that she was not carrying any of the luggage she swore to pack for her supposed departure. But I found a half-packed bag on the bed later that day.

I allowed myself a small sigh of relief. Our entire exchange had been forgotten already, despite the fact it had barely even been five minutes. Another silver lining. Any arguments we had now would go from a burning house fire to dying embers in the minutes it took for me to walk from one room to the other. But just because Reece had forgotten them so easily didn't mean that I could.

I felt a pang in my heart at the memory of Reece rejecting me only a moment ago. Oh, how easy it must be for her to let all of these negative memories go, but at what cost? In forgetting them, Reece had discarded all of the positive ones too.

As I made my departure that morning, Reece asked for a kiss goodbye. As I leant over and received the peck on the cheek, I was thrown back to twenty-five years before, remembering those times when Reece would bid me farewell before the start of our working day. Reece at university and me at the café and then later when I was in the police force and she had begun to teach.

My eyes began to sting because those memories seemed so far away now.

"Hey, just one more thing," she said as I turned away to hide my impending tears. "I love you," she added.

I think I cried from the moment I shut the front door all the way to the shop. How could half of me not love her, then the other half love her so fiercely that it destroyed me every time I saw her the way she was?

Chapter 7

A few months later
May 2032

After I fell into the vice-like grip of Alzheimer's, there wasn't much I could do. I couldn't speak, couldn't walk. I regularly soiled myself, and my food had to be cut up so small that it was practically pureed.

Lois and Jessie did their absolute best to take care of me, and I would always be grateful and proud of them, but I was not stupid. Even when I was in that "coma," as some people liked to call it, I think I knew in some untouched part of my brain that Lois wanted to leave, and who could blame her?

Back then, there were even laws in America that meant you could divorce your partner if they were as ill as I was, but those laws never did reach this side of the Atlantic. I guess they must still exist over there now, despite the fact that there's no reason for them anymore.

I expect that's true of a lot of laws over there; they became obsolete after everything that happened. There was nobody left to obey them.

In the three years following my diagnosis, Lois took me to the doctor several times, for check-ups and various tests, but there was always one appointment that stuck out to me. I found the conversation in that doctor's office hard to follow. The large black masses inside my brain had multiplied, and by then I was having a hard time recalling Lois altogether.

I don't remember the first time I forgot her, just like I don't remember forgetting any of my other memories or abilities. I just woke up each day, and these things were gone— one by one or as a cluster, all at once.

It was painful to me that Lois could remember this time very clearly. I knew it caused a lot of irreparable damage to see me like that and to be on the receiving end of my forgetfulness. But I never stopped loving her in those times; even when I forgot her, I liked to believe there was an untouched piece of me that was always hers. Kept safe in the depths of my heart where the Alzheimer's couldn't reach it.

But then it was so easy for me to love her because she never changed; she was always solid, secure, and dependable. She was always *my* Lois.

And who was I? I wasn't Reece. For a long time, I had stopped being Reece, and maybe I never got back to being her again. It's hard to be the person you once were when a trauma such as Alzheimer's has taken over your life for so long. Many of the survivors would tell you that. But I like to think that I reclaimed most of my old life. I know that I even reclaimed Lois's love for me eventually.

We went to our family doctor some time at the beginning of May in 2032. Lois had already been recommended AZ by the doctor on a previous visit. But she insisted on doing some more research on it before she agreed to anything. There were fleeting parts of this that I remembered, but I asked Lois to fill in the blanks.

"I've read online, but well…are you sure it works? It's hard to take in…" Lois had asked on her return.

Despite the research she had done online, some residual doubt remained. Maybe she didn't want to become too hopeful should the drug not work. But Doctor Thomas understood her concerns almost immediately. She told us about her other patients, patients who had taken the drug and had started walking again just recently already. She told us that we weren't alone in our doubts, that other carers had had similar thoughts, but she was sure that the drug was right for us.

I say that she was talking to "us," but what I really mean was that she was talking to Lois. By this point, my conversation skills had reached an all-time low. Nobody ever spoke to me anymore, and when they did, it was mostly in baby-like voices. Except for Lois and Jessie. I think they tried to talk to me as normally as they could. I expect they hoped that I might understand them, but they were wrong. I had reached a point in my Alzheimer's when you could have said anything to me and I would have nodded and smiled along with the conversation, completely oblivious.

"And once she takes it…that's it? She's fine? She'll come back to us, and she'll be cured?"

"Yes," the doctor replied. It was a simple response, and yet Lois bawled her eyes out after she heard it. I imagine it was a massive relief to her and a huge weight off her shoulders.

What she was thinking was that in a year, maybe even a few months, she would no longer have to take care of her ailing partner, and she would be free again. I would be free again. We would no longer be slaves to an incurable disease.

"Thank you so much," Lois said when she received the prescription slip, her eyes red and swollen.

"It's not a problem. I'll get to see you both in a few months with news of Reece's progress, I hope?" the doctor asked. She beamed over the top of her spectacles.

At the pharmacy, we sat and waited for our prescription to be processed. There was a buzz in the room, a buzz that came from Lois alone. It was full of excitement and anticipation. I could feel her practically bobbing in her seat, and the movement was making me feel ill, so I cast my eyes around the room as a distraction.

On the walls were various posters reminding patients about jabs and inoculations and pharmaceutical products that could be bought in store. But there was one poster that stood out from the rest. It was a huge advert for a new drug, and I remember it quite clearly because it was *my* drug. There were a few colour photographs of various people with captions saying their names and ages. There was one portrait that caught my eye: an American woman pictured with what looked like her granddaughter. The child was grabbing at her face; both of them had been caught laughing as the camera went off. Happiness beamed from the photograph, and it made me think of my own family.

The caption informed me that the woman's name was Joyce Williams, and she and her family were from Georgia. Throughout my recovery, these kinds of posters were everywhere, with similar photographs of happy families reunited after years of suffering. A blur of smiling faces and sickly sweet captions. But that picture—I still remember it now—is etched into my memory. Because that's the image that kept appearing on the news.

The pharmacist placed a small purple-and-white box onto the desk in front of us. Looking back, it seemed too small when you compared the size of it to the catastrophic years that followed; the proportions seemed all wrong. And maybe Lois knew it too, because her hands shook when she picked it up and placed it gently into her bag. So gently, as if it were a bomb about to go off.

And it was.

It was only when we reached our car, parked outside, that I realised we had even left the pharmacy. I had become used to these little black spots of blankness. My consciousness dipping in and out of the present without warning. But I do remember this part so vividly, which is strange because out of all that time when I was sick, why did my brain choose to remember getting into that car and all the moments surrounding it so clearly? Out of everything else?

The lock on the passenger door didn't work, and Lois had to climb over from the driver's side and release the catch from the inside to let me in. Had I known that the functionality of that lock would be so important a few years later, I probably would have reminded Lois about it as soon as I started speaking again.

But the lock was one of those things that didn't seem important enough to fix until you encountered a problem. Then it went forgotten about for another day. And then another and then another and then those days turned into weeks and then months. The lock is still broken.

"Did you understand any of that?" Lois had asked me at the time. She watched me expectantly, and I stared back at her for a few moments. Admiring her face. There were deep valleys creasing the skin around her eyes. Her auburn hair was flecked with grey and white streaks around her temples and in her parting. I thought that she was the most beautiful thing I had ever seen; it was that small piece of me that belonged to her bubbling to the surface again.

I couldn't reply out loud, couldn't tell her how beautiful she was, so I just shook my head. My forehead folded into a frown, but Lois placed a hand tenderly on my arm. Something about the touch was reassuring and comforting, despite the fact that her hand was cold. The comfort was a feeling I used to know well. But trying to remember it and recall the associated memories was like the moment a dream slips from your grasp when you wake up.

"You're going to get better," was all she said before her eyes began to well up again.

Later that day, Jessie and Lois helped me take my first and only dose of AZ. They then took me upstairs and put me to bed, despite my grumbled protests.

I felt drowsy almost as soon as I lay down, and within minutes I was asleep. I fell into a stupor so powerful that when I woke up completely for the first time since taking the drug, I felt more rested than ever before.

Chapter 8

May 2032

Michelle March woke with a start that morning. Her mouth was dry, and her head pounded with the beginnings of a hangover. Sunlight blazed through the window and scorched her retinas as she recalled the night before.

She had eaten alone at her favourite restaurant. The maître-d had reserved her usual table and had placed a chilled bottle of 2005 Chardonnay next to her place setting. Her table was tucked at the back of the restaurant, almost completely out of sight of the public. The staff were seen and not heard; they knew not to interact with Michelle unless offering her more alcohol or setting down her side salad in front of her.

A side salad, probably not the best thing to eat before drinking an entire bottle of wine and a waterfall of double gin and slim line tonics. But she wasn't going to load herself up with any carbs if she could help it.

She had stumbled slightly as she made her way out of the restaurant via the kitchen. Her '32 registration plate Jaguar sat boastfully, blocking the fire escape, just where she had left it. She had driven herself home, carefully avoiding the hot spots for police cars. Gone were the days when she could flutter her eyelashes and raise the material of her skirt to be waved on by a male officer. Laws were stricter now, and she was much older. There weren't many officers who were tempted by the patchwork of her varicose-veined legs.

When she had arrived home in record time, the house had been deserted, just as she had expected. Her husband was "away on business"…actually it was almost funny that he still attempted to use that clichéd excuse to thinly veil his various affairs. Who was it this week? Michelle had wondered out loud to herself. Would it be Cheryl, dark hair, dark eyes, with big tits? Or maybe it was Olivia, dark skin, black hair, with even bigger tits. Oh, he definitely had a type. But his type just wasn't his own wife.

Maybe he had found a new mistress entirely and had not yet clumsily revealed her identity to Michelle. She had given up snooping. The kind of lies that Rico spun often unravelled all by themselves.

On the way through the entrance hall, she had collected the unopened mail off the side table, where she placed it earlier before she left for work. She had made her way to the liquor cabinet and poured herself a double scotch. She paid little attention to the voice in the back of her mind that told her not to mix her spirits.

She had torn open the first envelope she came to, and two pieces of paper fell onto the counter. Her eyes had flicked down to the second piece of paper; the six-figure sum on the transfer receipt swam before her drunken eyes. She allowed herself a small, dry laugh when she read the accompanying letter.

> *Dear Ms March,*
> *Thank you for your continued public support for Medipharm Inc. We value the backing from clients such as yourself and look forward to your continued support in the future. Here's a little something to say thank you.*

She had pushed both pieces of paper away from her and stumbled towards her bedroom.

In the morning, Michelle crawled out of bed and bravely slouched downstairs. She made her way to the liquor cabinet again and poured herself a drink. Hair of the dog, she told herself, numbly throwing ice cubes into the glass.

It was hard to believe that her family life had once been the vision of perfection. She had juggled her career, her children, her husband, and her social life easily back then, and now it had all collapsed. Her children were grown adults, and their busy schedules had taken them far away from their mother.

At the thought of her children in different parts of the world living their lives, having forgotten about the woman who raised them, Michelle downed her drink and poured another. A triple this time.

At least she still had her career, she soothed herself. Who needed family when you were the most successful chat show personality of all time? And it was not like they didn't love her, because they did. But they were just busy, and it had never been their intention to leave her alone with their father. Did she really want her children to put their lives on hold for their withering old mother?

Withering. Old. That was not how she wanted to end up. Michelle steeled herself for another shot of scotch and slammed the glass on the kitchen's granite counter. The best granite money could buy, resting on the best handmade cabinets money could buy. In a house twice the size of what she and her husband needed.

At least he put the dozens of rooms to good use, a new room for each new whore he wanted to fuck.

She wiped a single tear from her cheek and poured herself another scotch. The letter from last night lay forgotten on the countertop.

⁂

A week later, a month later…I was not sure. On some days, time would pass unbearably slowly. Like raindrops sliding down a car window. And then on other days, it was gone in the blink of an eye.

However many days it was after I had taken the dose of AZ, I opened my eyes a fraction of a millimetre. Although my vision was blurred, I could make out a figure at the end of the bed. I sensed the weight of something or someone. A slight sag in the mattress where the weight was distributed.

I opened my eyes a little more. Just as slowly as before.

My pupils were shot to fuck, Lois delicately told me later. One was bigger than the other. I tried to focus on the person at the end of the bed.

I couldn't seem to remember who it was or if we had met before. As I stared, the figure let out a low moan. I could just make out its bared teeth in the dim light of my room. I cowered away from the noise and shut my eyes.

What felt like a moment later, I reopened them.

I had imagined it. The figure remained still at the end of the bed.

Nameless, but with an identity that I was too exhausted to find out. Hope of discovering who it was was given up easily, and I fell back to sleep. My eyes slammed shut like heavy blinds.

I would try again tomorrow, I promised myself, if the person was still there.

The figure watched me patiently but did not speak. Their eyes blue unseeing. Teeth clamped shut behind tight lips.

⋏

There she was, lying in bed, oblivious to everything that had happened. And here I was, an emptiness inside me that was so vast that it felt like I would never escape it.

She was going to get better, I thought to myself. And I was meant to be happy. I was meant to be excited. But somehow I couldn't be.

If you had asked me a year before what would I think or feel if Reece were cured, I would have told you that it would be the best day of my life. I would have leapt around the room, screaming and yelling with happiness. But those feelings felt so far removed from where I sat, at the end of her bed. My heart heavy.

I hadn't wanted her to take the dose. I hadn't wanted her to be cured.

It was Jessie who changed my mind. It was the hope in Jessie's eyes, the longing for the mother she lost long ago. And I couldn't deny her that. What kind of person would I have been to let the mother of my child die knowing I had the cure in my hands?

So here we were, Jessie over the moon. Jessie making lists about all the things we could do as a family when Reece was cured. Jessie singing, loud and out of tune but full of happiness. Reece, making the first trembling steps of a long road to recovery. Not even aware of what she had so narrowly escaped.

And me. Selfish me. Unable to love. Unable to summon any feelings of care for the woman I was supposed to have committed my entire life to.

What a difference a year makes.

Farther and farther I fell into unconsciousness. More time passed. It could have been months; it might have been years that went by, but I could not tell. Each time I seemed to wake up, I felt like I was more and more aware. My brain crawling to the surface of a deep lake. The exhaustion that weighed heavily on my brain and controlled my eyelids slowly lifted itself with each sleep-wake cycle that I went through.

I was yet to recognise the figure at the end of the bed, but I felt like I would soon. The figure's long auburn hair that fell past her shoulders was beginning to become more familiar to me. A flame bringing light to the darkness of my mind.

I felt a dull ache in my stomach, but I could barely recall what it meant anymore. My eyes flickered with determination, but they were not successful. They closed again after only a few seconds of working. The seconds were not long enough to absorb any of my surroundings.

They closed again.

The figure at the end of the bed remained patient, watchful, and entirely human.

Saanvi Singh dropped her car keys in the fruit bowl on the kitchen table and placed her handbag next to it. She hung her light jacket on the back of the kitchen door and went over to one of the eye-level cupboards. She opened it and pulled out a large packet of salted crisps and shut the door behind her. Then she walked into the living room next door.

She called out to her television to start up. After a moment's hesitation, it flickered to life, and she requested her favourite news channel. The machine obliged, and she took a seat on the sofa, tore open her bag of crisps, and began to eat.

A smug and satisfied grin spread across her face as she watched reporters and scientists alike gushing their admiration for her product. And all the news outlets were playing this same story; each and every one of them was hailing her work. She had finally done it. She was famous.

It went all the way back to her childhood, her face getting pushed into mud, her loose shoelaces getting trod on in a bid to trip her up. Ever since those days, she had promised herself that one day the whole world would know her name…and now they did. When she was growing up, she knew she could never be an actor or the lead singer in a band. She lacked the creative ability for either. But she had always had books. She had always been intelligent, and she used the tools that she had to get herself on that pedestal.

Now here she was, living in a North London three-bedroom house that she owned, driving a bright red Porsche with blacked-out windows that she also owned outright—no finance agreement in sight—working in a career that she adored. And most importantly, her name scrolled across the ticker at the bottom of every news channel in every corner of the globe. And it was her name that would go down in the history books. And fuck, didn't it look good? Didn't it just look like a name that was meant to be known, to be discussed, to be praised?

She blushed with pleasure at the idea of students all over the world revising her name in textbooks as they studied for their final medical-related exams. They would read excitedly and with rapt attention about the complete eradication of Alzheimer's. They would continue on to find out about how she came to lead the world to the greatest medical discovery since penicillin.

But…might they study how she did it? Which methods she used?

They would read about the mice…

Her mice.

The thought caught in Saanvi's mind, and her stomach swirled in fear. Her conscience opened its large and all-knowing mouth to speak, but she silenced it swiftly. The mouth snapped shut, and it slinked away to the back of her mind.

She was famous now, and that was all that mattered.

Part Two

Chapter 9

2032–2033

Dread filled me.

It was as if I had gone to sleep as a healthy person one night and had suddenly woken up the next day to find that my entire body was paralysed. My mouth opened and closed, but my words remained trapped inside the tomb of my chest. And I had no idea how long I had been like that.

It felt like forever, but then it also felt like not very long at all.

My mind had suddenly lit up. The lights inside me were ablaze with thought, and most of all, with hope. My once sluggish thoughts were now racing with the need to move, to get out of bed, to speak to somebody, and yet my body was an unwilling participant.

Each day, I opened my eyes and glanced over at the digital calendar mounted to the wall. Each day, I tested the limited movement of my limbs and the ability of my tongue. I began the arduous task of reforming myself and reclaiming those functions that had slowly withered away in the cavern of my mind. My brain felt like a painted canvas covered in a film of dust. Delicate strokes had to be made to brush away the dust without damaging what was underneath.

All the words I used to speak so freely and with such ease had to be relearnt. I had to start from the very beginning, finding the simplest of words to string together to make the smallest of sentences. It used all of my concentration to push them reluctantly out of my mouth. And it was exhausting. It made me want to sleep for days at a time, but it would also fill me with such a fierce determination that sleep was impossible too.

I just wanted to move, to walk, to talk, to be, to exist beyond the confinement of my bed.

Each time I woke, I could hear the noises of other people far away in another part of the house. They visited me sometimes, and each time they did, they introduced themselves. They claimed to be my wife and daughter, and they stared at me expectantly. This hopeful gaze that pained my chest.

After the tenth introduction, I finally began to believe that they were who they said they were. After the twentieth introduction, I wanted to holler at them that I already knew that and they could stop repeating themselves and they could stop staring at me with such pity. Though no matter how hard I tried, the words would not come.

The pair were patient as the days passed, and they always gave me encouraging smiles and nods. But each time

I could not speak to them, I sensed an undertone of disappointment in their reactions. Their expressions dropped, and their soothing noises became shorter and less enthusiastic. To them, it did not seem to matter how much I moved my limbs or forced expressions to form on my face. They wanted speech. They wanted my voice, my laugh, and my cries.

When I looked at the calendar one morning, I calculated that twenty days had passed since I had first become conscious. I noticed that I could raise my arms higher than before. I named the dull ache in my stomach "hunger" and tried to coerce my wife and daughter into giving me food.

On the thirtieth day, I found the power to move my legs up and down off the mattress, but they felt as though they were made of lead.

On the thirty-fifth day, I realised that I needed the toilet desperately, but my restricted movements meant I was unable to reach the bathroom. I soiled myself, and my bed sheets had to be changed. My wife did not even flinch as she stripped back the dirty sheets, and shame flooded me. She moved so methodically around the bed I realised that this had to be a regular occurrence.

But, my wife. *My wife. I have a wife,* I thought. *I'm married, and I have a child too.*

How long had we been married? How old was our child? Was she the only child we had? I strained my memory, trying to think if there had been anybody else in the house at any point.

When and how did I meet my wife? Had we been together long? Did we share the same interests? Listen to the same music? Watch the same films? Laugh at the same things? All of these questions swirled around in my head, begging for answers. I vowed to let each of them be known, if and when I could speak.

In a bid to find the answers, I clung to any glimmer of information I could. This wife that I had, she was an understanding person. She was patient. Her patience was so unyielding that each time I made a mess of the bed and she had to remake it, she did so without complaint. My wife was funny and smart. She had a perfect smile that threw me back to a time when I used to walk through the city streets and hold her hand as we cried with laughter, completely immersed in our own world.

Her hair was a golden red colour that became ablaze in the sunlight, like the fires on the fifth of November. The image of her hair reflecting that light made me think of coffee and books. Made me feel excitement and nerves all at once.

Her azure eyes told me the story of two women who met by chance in a café, whose paths intertwined over the months that followed until they knotted together, unable to be picked apart.

Lois, she said. My name is Lois.

⋏

Two hundred thirty-five days after I woke up on that first morning to find I was no longer in a coma, as I called it, I motioned to Lois that I needed the toilet. The action had been so light and felt so natural to me that I had barely noticed it myself.

I just nudged her arm and pointed in the direction of the bathroom. Lois, who had been lying on the bed alongside me reading a book out loud, had been overcome with excitement. She had practically screamed for our daughter to come upstairs, and the two of them hauled me out of bed.

Later that day, I leaned on their shoulders as they guided me downstairs. The three of us ate dinner together. I was served a pureed mess of vegetables and chicken with a toddler's plastic spoon to eat with. An oversize bib was tied around my neck to protect my clothing, and a plastic sheet lay under my chair to catch any fallen food. I considered the sheet to be slightly obsessive, but Lois, after noticing the frown on my face, had assured me that it was necessary.

The more able I became, the more I seemed to remember that Lois thought every minute detail was necessary.

In those days, my old thoughts and memories came back sporadically. Some came back with the pace of a pack of snails. They inched closer and closer to me, almost within touching distance, until finally they made sense. Others came back like bolts of lightning through a dark and dense night and needed very little prompting to restore themselves in my mind.

In the hours that I spent lying on my back in bed alone, I wondered what made these memories so different from the others and why they were so eager to be remembered first and without any assistance.

Some nights I woke up drenched in sweat, my heart beating furiously. Thoughts of panicked cries and locked car doors and shotguns firing. Images of an old lady and her granddaughter spinning around in my head. In the first image, they were happy. It was that poster from the pharmacy. In the second image, the little girl was dead, her throat ripped out. But the grandmother, her eyes were lit up in this incredible electric blue.

When I woke, I saw those eyes in the darkness of my room, starting back at me until I blinked and they disappeared.

Only once did my nightmares wake Lois up too.

"What are you thinking about?" she asked me softly as she caressed my damp face. I turned to look at her.

She lay on her side, the moonlight cast across her auburn and grey hair, which cascaded across the pillow. Her bare shoulder broke out from underneath the duvet. Her skin was as pale as mine was dark, and I compared the two tones in the half-light.

I opened my mouth to respond, but my mind stalled and the words failed to make it past my front teeth.

"One day, when we least expect it, you're just gonna open your mouth and quote the entire works of Shakespeare, aren't you?" She smiled. "Or on second thought, you never did like Shakespeare, so maybe you'll give us some Jane Austen instead."

Instead of "you," she said "yer," that Yorkshire accent so faint now, but I knew it was there. Even the subtlety of it then transported me back to my first year of university. My nostrils flooded with the strong smell of alcohol and the heavy rhythmic thud of music.

Lois laughed a hearty chuckle, a noise so infectious that I couldn't help but smile and think again about how absolutely breathtaking she was.

"Until then…I guess we'll just have to wait and make some educated guesses at what's going on inside that big ole head of yours," she added and gave me a playful pat.

Later that morning, when the moon had disappeared and the sun had taken its place in the sky, she rolled away from me and sat up. She pushed her arms upwards and took a long, satisfying stretch. I watched the muscles in her back ripple in pleasure and heard the clicks of her spine as it loosened itself for another day of work. I praised myself as I remembered without prompt that she was a police officer and had been for twenty-three years.

These were some of the little facts that my brain and my family had released to me over the passing months. They were small and incomplete, but they gave me an unquenchable thirst for more.

I wanted to wish Lois a good day, but I couldn't quite remember that part yet. I only knew that I was capable of movement, of using the bathroom unassisted. Hell, I could almost start eating solid foods without that goddam bib. All of which were fantastic victories to my family and me. But the three of us knew that each one of these was not as important as regaining my speech.

Above all things, I wanted to tell Lois I loved her. I wanted to ask Jessie how school was…or college…or about her job, if she even had a job yet. Was my daughter funny? Did she still get upset when faced with a stressful situation? Did she still need to be reassured? Who was it that reassured her now, if not me?

Was she smart? Did she get good grades? Maybe she had a boyfriend or a girlfriend. Maybe she didn't have either of those things, and that would be OK too. It would just be nice to be able to ask her. And be able to hold a conversation with her that wasn't completely stilted and one-sided. A conversation that wasn't full of awkward silences and my stares, trying to convey messages through only my eyes.

⋏

"Happy birthday, sweetheart," Lois announced and raised her glass. Jessie raised her own, and the two of them watched as I attempted to do the same with my plastic cup.

"Thanks, Mum," Jessie replied.

I mentally tried to guess her age. She must have been sixteen at least. She was taller; her shoulders were broader, and she had grown out her hair into a huge Afro. The low pitch of her voice indicated that there were no longer any elements of a child about her. Maybe she was seventeen or possibly eighteen.

Almost at once, Jessie and Lois entered into their own conversation. They attempted to include me by throwing me more encouraging looks and smiling at me, but after a few minutes, the conversation always went the same way. They became engrossed in each other's company; their looks towards me became less and less frequent.

It was infuriating to listen to, and I couldn't help feeling jealous. Jealous of their relationship and how much they had experienced together and how much they must have bonded over it. I was jealous that they could speak and I couldn't. But how was I meant to speak again without help when I had forgotten how to long ago? How was I meant to remember the way it felt to shout and scream and roar with laughter?

It was infuriating that nobody was teaching me any of that. And yet, they hadn't needed to teach me how to move again or how to walk or how to use the toilet, and here I was, doing each of those things.

I took a deep breath and tried to picture the words I wanted to say. I knew exactly what they were. I must have said them a hundred times in different orders and contexts and sentences. So why was it so hard just to get them out of my mouth? They were beginning to taste sour on my tongue with the effort of trying to speak. I wondered if it was this difficult for toddlers learning their first words. If so, I genuinely felt sorry for them and vowed to allow them more of my patience when they struggled to string a sentence together.

Determination rushed through me, and I opened my mouth. This would be it. This was the moment I would finally be able to speak. I could feel words rising from deep in my chest, but then just as they reached the very tip of my tongue, the words stalled and died before reaching my lips. Gone again.

I felt my mouth open and close like a goldfish trying to breathe out of water. Thankfully, Lois and Jessie hadn't noticed me yet. I couldn't bear their encouragement at that moment, knowing that I could only disappoint them when the words eventually failed to materialise. I watched on as they continue to speak easily. Their words slipped out so effortlessly, subjects covered, discussed, concluded, and moved on from in easy minutes.

I could almost feel the neurones in my brain fusing back together, paths recreating, the plaque disintegrating with each attempt to push my words out of my mouth. I practised the sentence twice more in my head, and then almost as if a light bulb had reignited, I knew I was ready.

You found that sometimes you could try every day for weeks and weeks to learn a particular piece of music or master a skill and then all of a sudden you wake up and it is there at your fingertips like you had known it all along.

"H-h-how o-o-old a-are you?" I gushed. It was a quick, muttered sentence, and I thought that maybe they wouldn't even understand my question.

The words fell out of my mouth in a jumble rather than in the coherent sentence I had practiced in my mind. My voice was lower than I remembered, and it was strange to hear it again for the first time in so long. I laughed inwardly as I realised that there was a slight Yorkshire inflection in there, something that I must have picked up from Lois in the last year. My palette susceptible to accents as it rebuilt itself. But it made me feel like my voice didn't belong to me at all. It was a voice that was too weak; it was far weaker than I remembered. So maybe they hadn't even heard me.

But they had.

Like a bullet, my speech shot a gaping hole through the conversation, and they whipped their heads around to look at me.

"What did you say?" Lois demanded, her eyes wide, her mouth a perfect O.

How easily she talks! I thought resentfully, before I could stop myself. What would I give to not have to think about each word so carefully before I spoke? Oh, how good it would be to have that carefree speech that every other human adopted.

"She asked me how old I was," Jessie whispered. "I'm eighteen. I'm eighteen years old, and I am your—"

"D-daughter, yes. I k-know," I stammered before she could finish. My face split into a grin; I had interrupted somebody! A feat I never would have thought possible again.

"Your daughter," Jessie and Lois repeated together, like they were the best two words they had ever heard.

The three of us didn't move. I guess we were all terrified that the spell might be broken if one of us even dared to.

We were too afraid to scream with joy in case it rendered me speechless all over again.

⁂

"As you are well aware, you were sent for a few tests last week. This was just to confirm what we already knew…" Doctor Thomas began.

Lois and I sat opposite her, and a large modern desk sat between the doctor and us. The desk was stacked with papers, disposable gloves, a computer, and a tub of antibacterial handwash. In the doctor's hands was a tablet device, and as she spoke, she flicked absentmindedly between two images.

She placed the tablet on the desk in front of us and flipped the first image so it was the correct way up for us to see it.

"This first image is one of the scans that we took of your brain during your diagnosis," Doctor Thomas indicated.

I recognised it already. I had seen it many times before, and what it meant had already been explained to me. In it there were dark patches, which the doctor had explained meant a decrease in brain activity. It didn't take a genius to work out that those dark patches were where the Alzheimer's had been taking effect. The parts of my brain that were visible appeared to have a blurred appearance; they too were dying off in the same fashion.

She swiped left on the tablet to show me the next image, and this one really caught my breath. When you compared the two pictures, you could see that my brain had almost doubled in size from what it had been when the Alzheimer's was at its worst. Of course, it would have been nice to see what my head had looked like before the Alzheimer's had shown up at all, just to satisfy my curiosity. But who needs a brain scan before there's anything notably wrong with their brain?

The brain in the second scan, the healthy brain, was almost unrecognisable. The black blooms of shadow that demonstrated the damage to my brain had been eradicated completely. My healthy brain was alive with pale grey tones; there were no shadows in sight.

"AZ reversed all of the damage that the disease did to your brain. See the difference in the two images? The plaques that Alzheimer's caused are now completely gone. Your brain is fully functional with no hint of the Alzheimer's ever being there in the first place. You could say that this brain is more efficient than it was before. That's the beauty of the drug. Not only does it completely destroy the disease but also rebuilds what was there in the first place *and* improves it. And in that respect it's a one-of-a-kind-type drug.

"Most cures can only seek to remove certain parts of a disease or rather the symptoms of the disease. And this is never really one hundred per cent successful because there is always a threat that it will come back. AZ is special. It's different, and I can't talk about it highly enough. Whoever created it did a fantastic job."

The feeling was indescribable. My heartbeat roared in my eyes. But I had to ask one last question, just to be sure. And I knew that Lois wanted to ask it too.

"So that's it? I'm completely in the clear now?"

"Yes, Reece. I am pleased to tell you that you are in remission. The Alzheimer's has gone."

⁂

Lois flopped into the seat next to me. The leather of the sofa let out a little shriek of surprise, and we burst into a fit of giggles. Our laughter was exaggerated after the night's festivities of wine and champagne.

"Hey," she said breathlessly after a few moments. Her eyes were wet, and she dabbed at them with a tissue from the box on the coffee table.

"Hi," I replied, wiping my own eyes with the end of my sleeve.

A moment of awkward silence passed between us, and Lois's eyes darted around the room and her leg shook with nerves. I wondered what she must be thinking about.

"I'm happy," she finally said. Her voice was a whisper, so low I only just heard it.

"I know. Me too."

"I wasn't…I wasn't happy for a very long time. I don't know—" she began.

"I know," I repeated. And I had known. I had known all along that I was not giving her what she needed.

"I'm sorry," she added helplessly. Her eyes searched the room again, as if what she wanted to say would be written on the walls or the furniture.

"It's OK. I understand," I soothed.

"But it's not. I was selfish. I wanted to leave," she stopped, and I waited.

My instincts told me not to speak. I knew Lois well enough to know that whatever she needed to say would come out of its own accord, and it didn't take long for me to be rewarded.

"I thought it was too late. I honestly did. When we discussed giving you the medication, I was against it. I thought if you came back, you wouldn't be the same person. It was selfish, I know. It was Jessie who convinced me. I saw the desperation in her face. She wanted so badly to have a relationship with you. I couldn't deny her that, and I'm sorry I ever thought that I could."

"It's OK, honestly," I repeated again.

"It's not, Reece," Lois half shouted. She leapt from the sofa and began to pace the room. "I want you to be mad at me. I was willing to let you go. I was willing to let you die for crying out loud. Punish me, be mad at me, anything!"

She crouched in front of me now, her body lower than mine, her eyes looking up to me, pleading.

"Lois, listen to me. There is nothing for you to be sorry for. You were desperately unhappy. You were confused, and you were hurting. I forgive you. I forgive you for wanting to leave."

Her head dropped, and she began to sob.

"I'm sorry. I'm so fucking sorry."

I dropped off the sofa and sank to my knees, taking her into my arms. She leaned into my shoulder, and her whole body shook with her sobs, but my arms stayed firmly around her. We stayed like that for a long time; it felt like hours, and my knees had begun to get sore, but I didn't want to let her go. I wanted to hold her until she finally believed that she was truly forgiven.

Finally, we broke apart, and I held her at arm's length. Her eyes were red and puffy, and her face was a bright pink, but fuck, didn't she look beautiful? I felt a sudden and irresistible urge to kiss her.

I leant forward and took her face in my hands. My lips found hers, and I kissed her with as much softness as I could manage. It had been so long since we had done this, but it reminded me of a time when we were younger, when we were at university and our love was only just beginning. I wanted more, but I held myself back. I tried to be gentle with my lips, not to allow too much pressure, but her lips felt soft on mine, and the feeling of them after all these years sent a shiver down my spine.

A thousand images raced through my mind. All of her. Her with no clothes on. Her lying in only her underwear on a bed in my grubby old flat. The milk-white of her skin glowing by the light of the moon. Her body glistening with sweat…

But she hadn't moved yet, and I felt her reluctance. I scolded myself for misreading the moment. She was asking for forgiveness because she still wanted to leave. She was still unhappy. Of course, how could I have got it so wrong?

Then, as I began to pull away, I felt her respond. She grabbed the material of my shirt and yanked me back to her, kissing me with the same ferocity that I wanted to show her. Before I understood what she was doing, I felt her hand on the back of my neck, forcing me even closer. She pulled me so hard towards her I felt myself losing my balance.

I let myself fall into her, and we rolled onto the floor. We broke our kiss, and I put out my hands to steady myself. I rested above her and took a moment to drink all of her in. Her hair fanned out beneath her like flames of a fire, and her eyes searched my face, seeking out feelings that she hoped I could reciprocate.

Impatiently, she tugged on my shirt again, pulling me down to her, and before I could register what was happening, she had my shirt over my head.

Chapter 10

January 2035
Georgia, United and Reformed States of America

Following the release of AZ, specialised clinics had appeared all over the country and all over the world. Community members who had taken the drug would be assigned to their local clinics and attend sessions that would aid them with their rehabilitation. The clinics were usually old refurbished care homes that used to hold Alzheimer's patients.

Since the cure was administered, the demand for care homes and carers became less. In some clinics, there were old relics of the forgotten age of Alzheimer's. Grab rails and grab handles lined some of the walls near steps and bathrooms. The remnants of hoists hung from ceilings, and in clinics with more than one storey, there were chair lifts.

Care homes for other ailments did still exist, but with the fall of Alzheimer's cases, the populations of these homes fell dramatically.

The most prestigious clinics offered a free counselling service to those who were still healing. Alongside the course, each centre offered physiotherapy, speech therapy, and appointments with a trained nutritionist. Each would aid the patients in their new lease on life. The course of counselling itself tended to last for a few months but would only start when the patient had regained the ability to speak. It was deemed completely redundant to those who had not yet relearnt this skill.

The particular clinic that Joyce Williams found herself at was fairly basic. It was not a refurbished care home but had instead been constructed specifically for the use of Alzheimer's survivors. It was a one-storey temporary building and would be torn down once the influx of patients had subsided, allowing the land to be reused for future projects. On the outside of the property, the walls and roof were completely white. Like most public buildings in the URSA, the white suggested a sleek and simple appearance. It decluttered the busy landscape of a city. And white paint was cheap—especially for buildings that had a short service life.

Colours were mainly reserved for residential spaces, and people always took advantage of their free reign of colour and building materials. Housing estates were now a mismatch of reds, blues, and yellows. The colours issued statements of wealth and luxury. In the early part of the century, houses were built in basic terms, and most were painted beige or cream. And internally the houses were decorated using only a small selection of wallpapers, carpets, and tiles. Now it was not very often that you found a house painted entirely white. The change in style mirrored the colourful boom of the 1960s and 1970s.

The inside of the clinic was painted a light blue in an effort to calm the patients. There were no TVs and no announcements that might distract them or hinder their recoveries. Only the bare essentials were needed to furnish the rooms. In the waiting room, there was a minimal amount of chairs along the walls, and only one small coffee table was placed in the centre. Where a stack of battered magazines would have normally lain, several handheld touchscreen computers replaced them. They were the approximate length, width, and weight of a standard book, only much thinner.

A few months ago, when she first started coming to the clinic, Joyce had snatched up one of the tablets after the receptionist directed her towards them. To her pleasure, she had found that there was enough on those tablets to ignite the spark of her memory.

On starting the tablet, she found that it had produced a timeline that began at the dawning of the twentieth century, commencing with the death of the English Queen Victoria and continuing on to the First World War. It went on in chronological order until present day, and with each year that passed, the tablets were updated. No matter who picked up the tablet and at what stage of the disease or recovery they were in, they could still bring their knowledge all the way up to the present day while they waited for their appointment.

By the time patients reached the stage of counselling, their brains were almost completely reinstated. And this tablet was the key to connecting the lines between the dots that they had formed in their own minds. Most of the information could be found on the Internet, but on the tablet it was compact and streamlined, and it was tailored specifically for the patients.

Which meant that the tablet included the history of Alzheimer's. In a separate application, the tablet displayed the discovery of Alzheimer's in the 1900s all the way up to its current unthreatening state. Now when the disease was diagnosed, it was no longer considered a death sentence; a single dose of AZ and the patient was cured. The tablet included notes about Saanvi Singh, the person credited with the discovery of AZ, a Briton who developed the drug. There was also an index of statistics and figures relating to diagnoses, deaths, and those in remission.

Like most Alzheimer's patients in remission, when Joyce first started attending the clinic, she could scarcely put the tablet down. Now she needn't bother to pick it up; she had read each and every minute detail on that tablet over a hundred times, and best of all, she could still remember all of it.

Until discovering the tablet, she had not known that Australia's growing tensions had erupted into a three-year civil war over the treatment of immigrants. She had not known that after the two Koreas had entered a "cold war," they had thrown aside their differences and now called their joint country something new entirely.

Most interesting to her was the news of her own country, the USA, which had adopted two new words into its name. It was now called the United and Reformed States of America. The "Reformed" addition symbolised the previous struggle of the oppressed in the country.

Twenty years before there had been an epidemic of racist and prejudiced murders by white police officers that had resulted in the largest uprising since the American Civil War. It led to the greatest country reformation in the entire world's history, greater than Australia's. Those who had been oppressed for centuries were now treated as equals and were considered "free" of the heavy hand of the oppressors.

Black people could finally walk past a cop on the street without fearing for their lives, and people in the transgender community no longer had to live constantly terrified of being attacked. Marriages between same-sex couples were practiced countrywide, and women were no longer treated as sex objects in the films they starred in or in their own lives.

The country had undergone such a staggering change that it was unrecognisable as the dark and desolate place it had been before. The people of the old America had stood strong in the face of all that was wrong with the country. Protests, some peaceful, some not, had formed the basis of the biggest civil rights movement in the country's history. The URSA was now ranked one of the best places to live in regards to equality in the entire world. And Joyce knew all of this from a few taps on the tablet screen.

To her, the exercise with the tablet had been so remarkable that she had spent the entirety of her first session with the counsellor discussing the most important events that she had missed while in her Alzheimer's "coma." Her excitement about learning these new things coupled with her new ability to talk had sent her mind and mouth into overdrive.

Joyce had first begun to talk when she was sixteen and a half months old. She had been declared "above average" for her age; however, her conservative parents had been unimpressed. Their disappointment that Joyce had not been a boy had far overshadowed her childhood prodigy status. They felt that Joyce's intelligence was largely of no use, as her primary goal in life should be to marry and eventually have children.

They were so certain that she would lead this life that they had not even bothered to save for her college tuition. But in a rebellious streak, Joyce ran away to college anyway, riding on a scholarship she had applied for in secret. She came back some years later with a degree, having not spoken to her family the entire time she spent away.

Almost a year after returning to Georgia, she became a teacher. And five years after that, she did finally get married, but she continued with her career before starting a family. She juggled both her job and her two children as they grew up and vowed that she would be a more liberal mother than hers ever was.

Despite the unconditional love that she had given to her children, they lacked the patience or attention in return to care for Joyce after her diagnosis of Alzheimer's. When she was seventy-one years old, she lost her ability to talk and was unwillingly thrust into a care home. She was left to live out the rest of her days in relative solitude, save for the other residents in her home. Her family reluctantly came to visit once a week at first, mainly propelled by guilt. Then their visitations became more and more sporadic until finally they made appearances only on special occasions.

Some years after she lost her ability to speak, Joyce was volunteered to enter the initial round of human trials for a new drug. At the time, the drug's name had not been publicly released. But if it had, the name would not have meant anything to Joyce, who had no concept of words or letters at all by this point. The organisers of the clinical trials had been in touch with Joyce's family and had offered them a deal they could not refuse.

Using their power of attorney rights, the family could enter Joyce into the trial for free. If it was a success, then Joyce would be cured of Alzheimer's. If the trial was unsuccessful, then Joyce would not be cured, and she would remain in the home as planned. The company that wished to enter her into the trials was so confident of their new drug that they offered to pay her astronomical care fees should the drug not serve as a cure. The family had had nothing to lose.

A month or so after the pharmaceutical company's offer was accepted, forms were signed and a one-off dose was crushed up and buried in Joyce's pureed dinner one evening. Shortly after that, she lost consciousness completely, or so she had been told. She was unable to remember anything at all from that time.

On awakening one morning, she felt an overwhelming sense of having missed something. After a few months had passed, she realised that what she had missed was four years of her life. She was distraught to learn that she had been absent from her daughter's wedding and the birth of her first grandchild, a baby girl. With a fierce determination to claw back all of the forgotten memories of her life, she began to walk again.

Joyce had walked all the way to the clinic today. Her gait was still unsteady, and her daughter had advised her against it, insisting that she take a cab. But Joyce could hardly bear the idea of not being able to use her legs after only just regaining control of them after all this time.

Joyce was seventy-six years old when she was able to talk again. Three years under the spell of Alzheimer's and three years spent coming out of it, and finally she was able to start rebuilding her life and reconnecting with her two children, their partners, and now her new granddaughter, Annie.

"Ms Williams?" a voice called. The familiar face of the receptionist bobbed around and tried to catch Joyce's eye. She indicated that it was time for her appointment.

With a rumbling stomach, Joyce stood from her chair and made her way slowly through the doorway into one of the small rooms that broke off the waiting area. She glanced around at the other patients she had been waiting with. Most were her age. Only a few were younger. But each of them had somebody accompanying them, a husband or a wife or a long-time partner.

Widowed shortly before her nineteenth wedding anniversary, Joyce never remarried. She instead chose to dedicate her life to her children, who were still in school at the time. It was a decision that Joyce had never come to regret. Devastated by the death of her husband, she found she could not fall in love with another person again even if she had tried. So she loved her children instead.

She had brought them up in the Georgian home that she had once shared with her husband. She worked long hours at a diner in addition to her teaching post to provide for them. Ed, who had worked on oil rigs in the Atlantic, had supplied enough money in his last will and testament and his life insurance to allow her and their children to survive comfortably for several years after his death.

She hadn't needed to get a second job or keep her teaching career on track with the lump sum that he had left her, but she kept them both anyway. She chose to save the money until their children were old enough to go to college and spend it on that instead. A local one, though. There hadn't been enough money to send them to any of the higher-league colleges parents always have in mind for their offspring.

An hour and a half passed and Joyce emerged from the therapist's office and made her way back through reception. She paused at the desk and made sure to sign herself out of the building. As she scribbled her name on the touchscreen in front of her, the receptionist tutted.

"Yet another one not answering the phone. I do wonder if these people even want our help," she fumed.

"What's that?" Joyce asked.

"Just some of your trial friends. They know they've got appointments scheduled, but they keep forgetting to turn up, and I can't get hold of them."

"I'll see if I can get in touch," Joyce suggested, trying to recall the last time she had spoken to one of her fellow survivors. She and a group of five others in the Georgia area had all been participants in the AZ trials. They had forged a bond amongst themselves and kept in touch through e-mails and phone calls. But it had been weeks since she last spoke to one of them, she realised.

"Thanks, Joyce. You have a good day now."

"You too."

Joyce exited onto the street and into the weak winter sunlight. She inhaled the cold, fresh air and headed towards home, a slight limp to her step. She walked slowly but with purpose in the direction of home, fully aware that her stomach was growling with impatience.

She passed a bakery on her way home and considered picking up a bag of doughnuts for her granddaughter. The bakery owner, Billy, stood in the doorway. He smiled, and she nodded in recognition but quickened her pace. Despite the fact that he was married now, he still harboured a soft spot for Joyce after all these years. He would often try to stop her and invite her in for coffee, but just like she had when they were growing up, she patiently declined his offers.

She couldn't fault him entirely, though. In the months following, he would be one of the first to defend her when the news broke that she had murdered a member of her own family.

Joyce arrived home to find her daughter, Barbara, in the kitchen, as expected, already working on dinner for the family. In the dining room, she found her son setting the table for the six of them. A high chair was parked at the far end of the table for the toddler. She soaked in the view, the idyllic family mealtime. An American dream. A tiny, misguided part of her wished she could have shared this moment with her own parents, but she pushed this thought away.

Joyce was dragged from her daydreaming by Barbara, who had been shooting accusatory looks at the shotgun that rested in the corner of the stair cupboard.

"You oughta get rid of this now, Momma," her daughter suggested casually in her southern twang. "It ain't legal to have that kinda thing no more."

"Now why would I wanna go and do a thing like that? I like that gun," Joyce retorted. This was not the first time her daughter had made the suggestion, and it was getting a little tiresome now that she no longer lived there. "It keeps me safe."

"I don't think you need to worry about that kinda thing no more. Besides, what if Annie finds it?" her daughter pointed out.

That's true, Joyce conceded internally. But she couldn't see why she should get rid of it entirely. It would make more sense to just put it somewhere safer.

"I'll move it tomorrow," Joyce replied. "That gun is twice her size. Poor angel wouldn't be able to lift it, let alone shoot the thing."

"It is still illegal, though, Momma. You could go to jail if the cops found it," her son chipped in. He was right. With the country's reformation came the nullification of several laws. During the reform and in 2025, the second amendment was deemed unnecessary, and citizens of the new United and Reformed States of America were no longer allowed to carry firearms. Not even law enforcement officers were permitted to.

In the twenties, lethal gun crime had reached an all-time high, and President Li couldn't ignore it any longer. Anybody who was found to have a gun after a year-long amnesty was sure to be arrested and imprisoned for possession of an illegal firearm. The following year, all law enforcement officers were ordered to hand over their weapons and surrender their gun permits. Naturally, since the removal and destruction of guns from society, the death toll for gun crime had been obliterated. Although Joyce agreed with the new laws, she and many others of her age had still been reluctant to hand over their weapons during the amnesty. A lifetime of relying upon a weapon for protection had dissuaded them from giving up their firearms.

"I just think there's better ways of—" Barbara began again.

"It's my gun, and I'm keeping it," Joyce snapped. Her daughter jumped with the sudden force of aggression from her mother and looked away. "It protects me, and I got every right to keep it here. It might not be a legal right, but as a person, I get to choose my own protection. And if y'all both recall, it protected you both just fine when y'all were growing up."

Neither responded. Her daughter feigned a sudden interest in peeling potatoes, and her son gave a noncommittal shrug and made a fuss of checking something on the stove.

"I'm gonna go sit down," Joyce added and left her red-faced children to continue the dinner preparations.

At supper, the six of them sat around the dining room table with loaded plates of food. Joyce finished hers in record time and made to stand to get herself a second helping from the kitchen.

"Another plate already, Joyce?" her son-in-law, Bob, asked. "You sure polished that one off quick! Maybe you should wait a minute..." He laughed.

She whipped her head around to face him. Her eyes were ablaze, and her lips were pulled back over her teeth in a snarl. Bob's laughing wavered.

"I'm hungry, and I want some more fucking food. Is that all right with you, Bob?" she snapped.

A deathly silence fell over the table except for Annie, who giggled at her grandmother. Bob stuttered an apology and looked to his wife and brother-in-law for some kind of assistance. His wife shook her head and gave a small shrug in reply, and her brother did the same.

When Joyce was out of the room, she waited and listened carefully for snippets of their whispered conversation to flow through a crack between the door and its hinge.

"She's been acting so odd recently. She's been really quite horrible. Honestly, Bob, she's not normally like this," Barbara soothed.

"I didn't mean to…I hope she…" Bob mumbled back. His voice had dropped its earlier confidence.

"Don't worry…" Barbara replied in the same calming voice her own mother had used on her as a child.

"It's probably just the medication she's on," Joyce heard her son add.

She frowned. That was a lie. She wasn't on any medication, and both of her children knew that.

Joyce stood at the kitchen sink and stared out the window that looked onto her unruly back garden. Now that she was more mobile and the weather appeared to be improving vastly with spring on its way, she wanted to spend more time in the garden. It had always been a favourite pastime of hers. She vowed that she would make a start tomorrow by digging up the weeds that had invaded her flower beds. Then she should cut the lawn back to a reasonable length…Maybe she would ask Bob to do it as a way of apologising. He loved gardening too, and it would be a great bonding exercise if they did it together.

She mulled over their charged encounter. She couldn't think what had come over her. One minute she felt absolutely normal, relatively calm in fact, and then the next it was as if she had been possessed. She couldn't believe how often rage bubbled up inside the cauldron of her body now, and on this occasion it had spilled over the edge. What had happened to her patience?

It wasn't the first time she had snapped at her family. She recalled a moment a few days ago when Barbara had suggested that they go grocery shopping together. It had only been a passing comment, a polite indication that perhaps they ought to stock up on some more fresh fruit and vegetables instead of the TV dinners she had been eating. But Joyce had practically roared that she could "do it her fucking self."

In her normal skin, Joyce would have jumped at the opportunity to go, just so she could spend more time with her daughter. And it had made sense to get more food, considering her large appetite at the moment.

Joyce's mouth watered. She was hungry again. She dashed over to the stove, and when she finished piling more onto the plate, she held it up to her face to take a closer look. Even in her state of increased hunger, she felt unsatisfied by the food she was about to eat. *Something is missing,* she thought. Her eyes began to defocus as she allowed her mind to drift to what she truly wanted.

*Something bloody, something tender...something...*she snapped herself out of the daydream and returned to the dining room. She hoped that this plate of food would finally quench her hunger for the day, although she was not optimistic.

During the rest of dinner, Bob would not meet her gaze across the table. He had run out of his comical anecdotes and no longer spouted praise about Joyce's "lovely home," an act that was getting quite boring anyway. The rest of Joyce's family members tried half-heartedly to start a new conversation, but the atmosphere had been scorched.

After dinner, Joyce was ordered to sit down whilst the rest of her family cleaned up the kitchen. Relieved to be by herself, she retired to the living room with her granddaughter. She placed her on the floor in front of the television whilst she listened to the noises of her children and their partners tidying the kitchen.

As Joyce watched her granddaughter, a warm feeling of love enveloped her. Annie's fat fingers grasped the toy cars as she played with them on the living room floor. She made animated car-like noises and lifted them into the air above her head. She mimicked the screeching of tyres and the explosions of the cars crashing together. Joyce cringed as she tried to imagine never knowing her granddaughter.

After a while, she leant down and picked her up from the floor. She placed the child on her lap. Annie looked up at her grandmother, and her face broke into a toothless grin. She dropped the cars onto the floor with disinterest. She pointed at Joyce's features excitedly, and the two of them erupted into fits of giggles. They could have spent hours like that, just staring at each other and enjoying each other's company.

Joyce recalled the aftermath of taking AZ and then when she finally became lucid enough for her family to interact with her and receive a response. She thought of her daughter's description of Annie and how she said that she was "completely obsessed" with her grandmother already.

From the moment Annie had laid eyes upon Joyce she hadn't left her alone. Perhaps it had been the similarities in their behaviour that had forged such a bond. At the time, neither of them could walk or talk, and both of them ate using plastic spoons with paper bibs around their necks.

While others had shied away from Joyce's deteriorating condition, Annie had embraced it in a way that only a child could. Children seemed to be unscathed by society's high expectations. Rather than pitying Joyce because of the memory of what she once was, Annie saw her as how she was now and loved her for it.

A sudden flash of hunger came over Joyce again, and her mind attempted to wander to the same place as before. She beat it back into submission. She leaned in to inhale Annie's sweet toddler smell, trying to distract herself. She kissed the top of Annie's smooth forehead. *How could I miss this?* she wondered to herself. All that time she had been under the spell of that dreadful disease and Annie had been right there in front of her. She didn't think she would ever be able to forgive her own mind for not being competent enough for Annie's birth and those first two years of her life.

As Joyce's mind ticked over like an old, faithful car, Annie reached out and patted her face heavy-handedly. Joyce could feel her granddaughter's tiny fingers as they poked and prodded at the fleshy surface of her own face. Joyce smiled, and Annie seized her chance to begin a fresh assault on her grandmother's false teeth. It had always been fascinating to Annie, the idea that a person could just "remove" teeth. She was always so drawn to her grandmother's set.

⋏

Joyce's legs jolted beneath Annie, and she shrieked with pleasure at this new game her grandmother had discovered. She hammered her tiny fists on Joyce's chest to ask for more. Joyce let out a second spasm so fierce that it almost knocked the toddler to the floor, but Annie still screamed with excitement at each new jolt.

Unperturbed, she carried on with her exploration of her grandmother's face. She had not noticed Joyce's fingers as they clenched and unclenched and could not understand that Joyce's shudders were involuntarily. Her fit carried on…and all the while Annie was completely oblivious. Her childhood naivety, once so endearing, had become a fatal flaw.

If there had been anybody else in the room that day, things might have gone very differently. Nobody was there to witness Joyce's expression transform from adoration to frenzied hunger, except for a two-year-old child. The toddler was too small to react when a guttural growl sounded deep within Joyce.

The toddler, who finally noticed her grandmother's strange behaviour, folded her face into a look of concern. The fold in her forehead deepened as she noticed her grandmother's peculiar new eye colour. Her eyes, which were once a warm dark brown, had transformed into a cold and striking electric blue. Entranced by the new colour of her eyes and so trusting of her grandmother, Annie remained completely unaware of the danger she was in.

So mesmerised she was by the eyes that she barely even whimpered when the hand that caressed her grandmother's wrinkled and sagged face was clamped between Joyce's teeth. It was torn off in a movement so fast it could have come from a person half her grandmother's age.

Annie's eyes widened, and her mouth opened to let out a louder and more terrified scream this time. But with a primal and animalistic instinct, Joyce silenced her. Her jaws, having left the stump of Annie's arm, were at her throat. She tore it free of the body. Overcome with a carnivorous hunger, Joyce began to feast upon her granddaughter's now limp body. She ripped off chunks of her skin and swallowed them whole. She buried her face in the bloody mass of the child's neck and emitted a half roar of satisfaction.

It was at least ten minutes before Joyce was finally interrupted, and her own daughter discovered the assault. Joyce's hearing, not quite as attuned as her sense of smell and desire for human flesh, did not pick up her daughter's entrance into the living room. So consumed in the frenzied hunger, she did not notice her daughter's harrowing scream. Neither did she catch the distinct sound of a gun being loaded. Her own gun, once there to protect her young family while she had brought them up alone in a dangerous world. It was loaded and pointed at her head.

Later, witnesses recalled hearing a succession of gunshots, one after the other, but despite the mild weather of that day, they blamed the loud bangs to a thunderstorm. Not one person was willing to believe that somebody in their community would use a gun, and so the gunshots were not reported to the police at the time.

Through fear of being caught in possession of a firearm, Barbara and her brother did not report the incident properly until much later.

On the day of the attack, Annie was taken to hospital where it was claimed by her family that she was attacked by a stray dog. She had not survived and was declared dead on arrival. The doctors who examined her did not find it strange that the teeth marks on the remains of Annie's skin bared no resemblance to that of a dog.

Word about the attack did not reach outside the small suburban town until months had gone by and whispers of Joyce's disappearance had finally invoked police interest.

By then it was too late.

It no longer served as a warning.

Chapter 11

Eleven years earlier
May 2024

At 7:00 a.m., Saanvi Singh entered Medipharm's Kingston-based laboratories by using the thumbprint scanner mounted on the wall next to the staff entrance.

When she arrived at her office, she began the long and unrelenting process of checking her e-mails from the weekend. She placed a cooling cup of coffee on the desk next to her and called out to her computer to initiate start-up.

As she waited, she took a minute to admire her office, which at the moment was untidy and cluttered. Stacks of paperwork and open folders full of half-read notes covered what available surface there had once been. A tablet unlocked on her desk was open on a page that had the simple title "AZ." Her eyes strayed to her in tray where there was a pile of yet-to-be-opened envelopes.

She allowed herself a sarcastic eye-roll as she marvelled at how prehistoric the postal system was. She tried to imagine how it had ever managed to survive the digital age. There were still some clients of hers, greying, old, and incompetent, who were reluctant to fully make the switch over to the use of e-mail. To Saanvi's relief, these people were a dying breed.

Others used the postal service simply because they enjoyed the novelty of writing long, handwritten letters to one another. Saanvi often refused to indulge these kinds of people and replied to their letters via e-mail, much to their disappointment. Unless they were letters offering her sponsorship and huge sums of money. Then, of course, she had no choice but to humour her correspondents.

Despite the progression of the digital age, Saanvi's computer took longer than usual to start itself and even longer to open her e-mails. It stuttered over her instructions, but its lack of speed was nothing new. Saanvi had meant to go over the machine herself and pluck out any of the unnecessary files for a few weeks, but she lacked the time. And she was so reluctant to allow anybody else access to her computer that she completely refused to request an IT technician to check it over for her. It would have to wait.

Saanvi used her index finger to scroll aimlessly through her e-mails. She gave each subject line and the sender a brief look-over first. She would make a more thorough examination of each of them a few minutes later. She deleted the couple that had evaded her spam blocker, and she refused to even open the six or seven that appeared to be from local charities asking for donations to their "worthy cause."

A message notification in the corner of her screen caught her eye. One new e-mail had just arrived. Straight away, she tapped on it using her finger and could see it was from one of her laboratory technicians and students, Brendan. The e-mail contained only one line of text, but her heart rate trebled in speed at the mere sight of it:

Need to go over some of my notes with you; 3:00 p.m., your office?

Although Saanvi was sure she was alone, she still took a hasty look around. No, it was just her and her e-mails. Heat spread up her neck and face. She shook herself quickly, and although the meeting was hours away, she self-consciously rearranged her skirt and blouse and smoothed down her long, thick black hair. The e-mail triggered an unreasonable nervousness that she wasn't used to somewhere in her stomach.

In a bid to calm her nerves, she reached for her coffee and took a sip. It was far too bitter for her, and for the third time already that morning, she wondered if her diet was such a good idea. What she would have done for a little sugar in her coffee at that moment; the sweeteners she had used didn't quite do the job. And the bland porridge and peanut butter combination she ate for breakfast was not fulfilling its promise of having satisfied her appetite. She already felt like she would need to eat again soon, and she had only consumed the porridge an hour ago.

That was the price she had to pay for her imminent fame, though. She knew that when her cure for Alzheimer's went global, she would be the most celebrated person in the world, and if she was going to be appearing on television, she needed to look her best. That included losing a few of the extra pounds she had gained during her last relationship. She pictured herself thinner, thin enough that she could see her bones protruding just below the surface of her brown skin.

She closed the e-mail from Brendan and continued to flick through the remaining two hundred that had accumulated over the time she had been away from her computer. The subject of one, received on Friday at 4:34 p.m. announced: "Well done!" At once she recognised the name of an old school friend and somebody she would rather not have had correspondence from. Despite this, her eagerness to hear praise got the better of her, and she double tapped on it. The e-mail filled the screen:

> Hi San,
>
> So sorry I havent got in contact sooner. Been v busy with some upcoming projects (will have to meet up and have a chat soon!) just wanted to drop you a quick line and say a massive congrats for your recent work! Heard all about it at a recent pharmaceutical conference in NYC—I'm there most weeks of the year now I might as well be a US citizen ha ha ha!

Of course if it wernt for bob and the kids I might have moved out there already. Alice and adam are 8 now can you believe it. Alice has taken up ballet and adam is a swimming champ at the local pool!

Hows your love life? Still seeing frank? I suppose youve been too busy for all of that—of course I always said that you would do well. Even when we were kids. Who knew I would be just as successful too AND with kids and a husband to boot!

Can't wait to hear more about the fantastic stuff u have been doing, would love to work with u. We have to catch up asap. Hop on a plane and get out here! Or if u can wait I'll be back in a few weeks. Fancy a coffee? My treat!

(Dr—im a doctor now!) Amelia xxxx

Attached to the e-mail were two accompanying images that were related to the subject matter. There was a picture of Amelia and her family on her graduation day. A skinny woman (Amelia) with cropped black hair underneath a square academic cap, a lanky, pale man (Bob) with glasses that made his eyes look like a crab's. And her two children.

The second picture, one of Adam and Alice together each holding their respective medals for their sports achievements, both sporting her jet-black hair. Amelia stood between them, her arms draped across their shoulders. She gave a smug and satisfied look into the camera. Saanvi's stomach swam with nausea as she reread the e-mail.

When she reached the closing lines again, Saanvi was stupefied as to how somebody who was a qualified doctor could forget the most simple of punctuation marks. She wondered which university had the pleasure of granting her with a doctoral degree. Probably Amelia hadn't even gone back to university but had bought her degree from some shady website.

It had been two years since she and Amelia had last spoken and for good reason. Saanvi found the woman absolutely insufferable, and even when they were at school together, she had had a hard time keeping her patience in check. But since they had graduated their first years of university together, Amelia had progressed from being mildly big-headed to downright obnoxious, and her behaviour had become unbearable. And now that she was a doctor too, her presence would be all the more agonising.

Amelia seemed to have understood and accepted Saanvi's slow drift away from their friendship. But predictable as ever, she couldn't resist an opportunity to boast. Especially about her God-awful children, who were just as insufferable as her, if not worse.

That was something Saanvi had always been thankful for—her complete lack of maternal instinct. Kids were not something that she had ever considered. Despite Frank's protestations, she had always been focussed on her career only. There was no room for children or even marriage. Perhaps this difference of opinion had led to the inevitable demise of their relationship.

Saanvi couldn't say that she was upset or surprised when they had broken up last year. She had become increasingly distant and was rarely home. Then one night after staying at the labs until almost midnight, she came home to find half of Frank's stuff missing. A note on the table in the kitchen claimed he "couldn't take it anymore." Saanvi knew that he had expected her to chase after him, but she hadn't. Her interest in Frank had been very minimal even at the start of their relationship, and by the end, it was practically non-existent.

Relief was all she had felt when he broke off the relationship; she only wished he had done it sooner.

Of course, bragging was not all Amelia wanted to do. Saanvi had no doubt that this e-mail had been sent with an agenda attached along with the two family portraits. But even the mere thought of this was incomprehensible to Saanvi; the project was her child. She didn't need her own flesh and blood because she had all the family she needed right in her career.

She was the one who had been researching Alzheimer's for the past however many years. She was the one who had spent nights sleeplessly analysing the data she had accrued over those years and at the expense of her relationship. And she was the one who spent even more sleepless nights tending to her mice. She ensured they were well fed, well watered, and had had plenty of exercise, all so they would be in full physical fitness and ready for the tests that had awaited them.

Hell would freeze over before Amelia would be invited to partner the further development of this drug, Saanvi thought. Especially now that they were on the brink of human trials. Her mice had done well. They had granted her the successful results that she had been waiting for. And as the virus was about to undergo the most extensive human trials in America, they were about to give her the level of fame that she so desperately chased all these years. Did she really want to share that with Amelia?

As she sat in her office and scrolled through her e-mails, miles away doctors were telling their patients and their families about clinical trials of AZ. They were targeting the nursing homes especially. Desperate families who would do anything to cure their ailing mother or father were almost guaranteed to accept any offer of a possible cure. But it wasn't just a "possible" cure. It was *the* cure. It was an exciting time for medicine. Saanvi yet again pictured herself on stage, receiving award after award for her hard work.

As Saanvi flirted with the possibility of inviting Amelia to visit, not to allow her participation but to be an observer, she had the sudden urge to visit her patients in the lab next door. After all, the recent success that Amelia had referred to in her e-mail was down to these patients. These mice were famous in the medical world; they would change everything for human beings all over the globe, and they wouldn't even know it. They didn't have the slightest comprehension that they weren't just average domesticated mice.

She pushed herself back from her desk and announced to her computer that it was no longer required and should resume standby mode. After an initial stammer in performance, the screen went black. She picked up the tablet from the counter next to her and excitedly power walked into the adjoining room and shut the door behind her. Five rows of small glass tanks were housed in one large block across the back wall of the room. In each row there were ten tanks, and in each tank there were ten white mice. They were almost entirely identical.

On entering the laboratory, Saanvi paused. She held her nose as it was assaulted by a pungent, rotting smell. She reluctantly crossed the room and peered into the first glass box mounted to the wall, Box A. She threw down her tablet, and on closer inspection and after making two thorough counts, she saw that there wasn't quite the amount of mice she was expecting. In fact, there appeared to be only about seven… and a half of them. Although the half was making a very good attempt at trying to be whole. Its front half seemed to be perfectly fine. Its two visible paws clawed at the sawdust that lined the bottom of the cage in an attempt to escape. Its back half, however, was non-existent, and its tiny entrails protruded from where its back legs should have started.

It was then that Saanvi noticed that this mouse was no longer white at all. Its fur, which once had the immaculate purity that only animals seem to have, was now bright red in colour. She looked around at the other mice and saw that their fur also had patches of red; some were completely covered. The mice were behaving erratically; one mouse appeared to be feeding off a second curled up in the corner of the cage.

Its tail twitched furiously as it tore, almost tiger-like, into the flesh of its friend.

Blood. The mice were covered in blood.

Another mouse ran from one side of the cage to the other. It hurled itself at the glass panel in a bid to break free. As it made another attempt to smash the glass close to Saanvi's face, she took a startled step back, seeing its blue eyes.

Blue eyes...but hadn't they been pink before? The remaining mice, grouped together, were all squeaking profusely. These were not the sounds of normal mice, Saanvi decided after considering their pitch. Between when she left her office and the lab on Friday night and returned to it on Monday morning, her mice had changed from the serene mammals they had once been. They were crazed cannibals, and they spoke to one another in a language that wasn't similar to their old dialect.

She turned her head slowly to take a look at the cages that remained; each box revealed a similar scene. Dead mice, half-dead mice that clung to life, mice that had been torn limb from limb. Their miniature intestines were mixed into the sawdust, and their blood had been smeared across the glass doors of their prisons.

When could this have happened? Saanvi thought to herself. Her initial suspicions were that the mice have been tampered with. Somebody must have sneaked in over the weekend and sabotaged her experiment. *Was it Brendan? Does he have a reason to do it? Does he know that I don't love him?*

Did he even know about the mice? These particular trials were over; the mice were no longer needed. Anything that happened to them would not affect the human trials.

The mice are no longer needed, she thought again. They had been waiting to be destroyed.

She addressed the thumbprint panel embedded in the wall next to the door into the lab. The display revealed only her most recent entry and her exit at 9:00 p.m. on Friday. The mice could not have been touched. Her second thought was a crushing blow of a question and one that she did not immediately want to address: If the mice were not intentionally tampered with, then what would this mean for her drug and the human trials?

If what the mice were experiencing was a genuine side effect of the drug she gave them, then AZ would not survive the human trials. Or rather, *humans* would not survive AZ and its trials. She would have to stop the trials from going ahead before they caused any further damage. But that would mean years of research would have amounted to nothing. She would have to start all over again. And if she were to let the trials continue and humans suffered the same fate, then Saanvi would be blacklisted. She would never be able to participate in finding a cure for Alzheimer's again. Unless...

There was a possibility that the drug might not have adverse reactions on humans. Just because the mice had not succeeded didn't mean that the humans couldn't. The human body and its immune system were built entirely differently to that of a mouse. That was the whole reason human trials had to take place and why tests on animals couldn't be solely relied upon for a drug that was meant for the human species.

Nobody had to know.

The panel had revealed that nobody had come in or out. To reassure herself further, Saanvi checked the cages. The food bowls were completely empty, and there was barely a drop of water in the bottles. Aside from the blood, the cages were filthy. Nobody had tended to the mice except her. She was sure of it. And she wouldn't have been surprised if people didn't even know the mice were still here at all.

She peered into one of the cages again. The blood in there was a day old at the most, she thought. If one of her colleagues or students or even a cleaner had been in to check on the mice, they would have raised the alarm almost immediately. That meant that she was the only person who could have seen this grisly outcome.

Saanvi picked up the nearby tablet next to the cages, and it came to life automatically. She used her finger to double tap on one of the various files on the home screen. Inside the file named "AZ" was all of the data she had recorded since the animal trials had begun. Months of research, pages and pages of notes. She scrolled to the bottom of the document, typed the date, and quickly jotted down the new characteristics of the mice.

- Mice appear to be aggressive in behaviour
- Demonstrating cannibalistic tendencies
- Subject 1011 in Box A exhibiting a psychotic episode

To the bottom of the document, Saanvi added several pages of notes, and as she typed, she peered into each cage a second and a third time in case she had missed anything. When she felt that she had written enough, she saved and closed the file and placed the tablet back on the counter.

She walked over to a large floor-to-ceiling window that looked out on the grounds of Medipharm's offices and laboratories. It was still early, and despite the fact that spring was well under way, a light fog lay over the lawns and flower beds. Saanvi rested her forehead against the cool glass and allowed herself to consider the future. She shut her eyes.

After an hour, she exited the lab and waited on the other side of the door until it closed with a hiss behind her. Once she was sure the door was firmly shut, she double tapped on the touch screen next to the thumbprint access panel. When prompted, she typed in her personal access code and opened the settings option on the screen. She disabled the access into the laboratory to everybody but herself.

The digital clock on Saanvi's computer screen told her that her visitor was three minutes late. She used the extra minutes to check her hair a few more times and to smooth down the creases in her blouse. She leaned casually against her desk and tried to listen for any approaching footsteps beyond her office door.

At 3:06 p.m. there was a soft knock. Saanvi leapt from her perch, and after a moment of hesitation to compose herself, she pressed her thumb against the panel and allowed the door to open. Brendan slipped easily through the gap, and despite his height, he didn't need to duck to get through the doorway. His blond hair swept back from his face in a look that suggested he didn't need to take much time on his appearance, that his good looks came naturally.

Saanvi motioned her thumb across the scanner a second time and set the door to "lock." There weren't many people who had the authorisation for entry to her office, and even fewer would use the access they had been granted. But she couldn't take the chance.

Saanvi turned back to Brendan, and they regarded each other for a few moments. Paired with blue jeans, he wore a crisp white-and-blue-pinstriped shirt under his white lab coat. A small smirk played across his thin lips, and he raised his eyebrows expectantly, though Saanvi did not speak.

"I'm meant to be with Doctor Morris right now," he began.

"Well, don't let me keep you," she replied.

As she spoke, she took a step forward and placed her hands on his shoulders. She could feel the taut muscles as they threatened to burst through his white coat and too-tight shirt. His heart rate quickened under the material of both. In turn, he pressed his hands firmly on either side of her waist. Her frame was so small that his hands practically engulfed her entire midsection. He had tried and failed to convince her to drop her fad diets; she was already small enough.

"He's an idiot. And your lessons are much more fun." He gave her a doe-eyed stare, and she found herself recoiling. She recalled a year ago when she promised herself "a bit of fun." It would be harmless. And it still was, at least for Saanvi. Brendan, however, seemed to have other ideas. It was the downside of having what you could loosely call a relationship with somebody younger than you. He was so naïve and so gullible. He held on to the belief that they would be together forever.

After only a few weeks of their extracurricular activities, he had suggested "going public"—a horrifying possibility that repulsed Saanvi, even now. As lonely as she was, Saanvi was not stupid. If she revealed the fact that she was sleeping with one of her students, then there would be disastrous consequences. He didn't mean enough to her to warrant the possible ruination of her career. Especially now that the human trials were about to begin.

She would just have to wait it out with Brendan. She would act coolly towards him, become distant. Then perhaps through lack of encouragement, he would find his own feelings slowly dissipating, and he would leave her alone. Hopefully he would make his own decision to break it off with her. Of course she would pretend to be heartbroken, and she might even plead with him to stay to appear more convincing. But in private, she would rejoice that she was finally rid of him, and unlike Frank, she hadn't even needed to break his heart in the process.

This would have to be the last time they met, she told herself. After that, she would put her plan into action. She would tell him that she was too busy to take his calls or to agree to his meetings. And without access to her office, he would not be able to arrive unannounced. Of course he would be hurt at first, but he would soon realise it was for the best, that staying in love with her would only cause him more pain farther down the line. She would need to have a clean break from him if she wanted to avoid the prying eyes of the masses when the drug became public.

Barely half an hour later, Brendan allowed the door to shut behind him. At its close, Saanvi buttoned up her shirt quickly and reordered herself. She shivered with mild disgust at the moment that they had just shared.

She had ushered him on his way quickly, hinting that she was too busy for these kinds of exchanges. She had sowed the seed of doubt in his mind already. Hopefully it would not come as too much of a shock to him when she suddenly withdrew from their encounters entirely in the next few days.

Her face glistened with sweat, and she wiped her forehead gently with a tissue from the box on her desk. She carefully reapplied her makeup, using the compact mirror that she kept in her purse.

As soon as she was dressed and looking presentable, she marched back to the lab. She checked the access panel. No entries and no exits, the panel informed her. She tried to reassure herself again that these mice were meant to have gone weeks ago, straight after the experiments were completed and the results published. Why would anybody check on what they presumed would be empty cages?

The mice, so lively and erratic only hours ago, were already dead. Their emaciated bodies were covered in scratches and open wounds. Saanvi wrinkled her nose as she approached the cages.

From one of the white surrounding cupboards, she pulled out a bright yellow hazmat bag and a pair of thick plastic gloves. One by one, she delicately picked up the rotting mice and threw them into the bag. With each one, she tried to hold back the disgusted and disappointed cries that meant to escape from her mouth.

When she had finished, she caught a glimpse of her reflection in one of the large windows. Her carefully reapplied makeup had run down her face. Her eyelids were blackened by her smudged mascara. Her cheeks were slightly pinked in her attempts to control her tears. She tried to compose herself for what felt like the hundredth time that day and peeled off her gloves. She threw them into the bag, which she tied tightly with a double knot. She then threw the entire bag into the matching bright yellow bin.

She produced the tablet, opened the document, and scrolled to her notes from earlier that day. She highlighted the entire three pages of extra notes she had added and deleted them all. She saved the document again, which overwrote any existing and damning notes that were there previously, and stored the tablet back on the counter.

Saanvi decided that now that the original results had been released, and the human trials would begin soon, the publishing of these notes could be catastrophic. Those mice had successfully passed all of the trials, and they should have been disposed of weeks ago. How was Saanvi to know that they would develop such strange behaviours?

She pictured herself with an expression of innocence when questioned about the behaviour of the mice. "How was I to know?" she cooed quietly and fluttered her eyelashes. *Perfect.* People would believe anything that came out of her mouth if she just kept the disguise of complete ignorance and gave them her big, brown-eyed expression.

Once she had exited the lab and given herself enough time to reapply her makeup for a third time that day, she scrolled through the directory on her phone. She sent for the most unquestioning of her lab technicians. Somebody she knew would be too terrified to speak up.

On the technician's arrival, she informed her that the mice in these cages had begun to rot and were stinking out the entire lab. She selected her most penetrating stare and asked why nobody had thought to clear them away. On cue, the technician turned bright red with embarrassment and attended to the empty cages at once. She mumbled an apology as she passed Saanvi and vowed that the cages would be cleaned immediately.

Saanvi paused and watched the girl's shaking hands as she emptied the soiled sawdust into a yellow bag. Once she was sure that the technician was suitably embarrassed enough that she wouldn't talk to anybody of importance about it, lest her incompetence be known, Saanvi left. The door that divided the laboratory and her office closed softly behind her just as the tears she had managed to stem began to spill down her face again.

Chapter 12

Eleven years later
April 2035
Adelaide, New Australia

"We've received a missing person report from a family in Sydney. Parents were meant to come and visit last week but never showed up, not answering their phone. They live out in the sticks, 'bout an hour outta the city. Any chance ya can go and check it out?" Sergeant Walters asked without looking up from the papers strewn across her desk.

"A week ago and they only just called the cops?" Officer Brenly raised his eyebrows, but Walters kept her head bowed. She let out a sound of exasperation but didn't let her pen falter from the page.

"We got a duty of care to check on these people and see if they're all right. They might have gotten into some kind of trouble. Just go and check on them this arvo. It's a slow day today, and it's something you can't bugger up too much." Her voice rose; the increased friction in the room sent the back of Brenly's neck prickling with sweat.

"Yes, ma'am," he mumbled. He knew better than to question her further. His actions last week had already landed him in hot water with her and the board. He began to turn to leave the room, but just as he reached the door, Walters spoke again. She had finally broken away from her work to give him a level gaze.

"And Brenly?"

"Yes, ma'am?"

"Take that waste of space Harrison with you, would ya? And try not to get yourselves killed. That shouldn't be too difficult for you, although I wouldn't mind if you proved me wrong," she spat.

Brenly shrunk out of the office, his face burning. He heard a cackle of laughter as he shut the door behind him.

An hour later, Brenly and Harrison rode in their marked squad car together, passing through the outer city suburbs. For the first few miles, they drove in silence as Brenly navigated the deep potholes that lined the streets like landmines. Immune to the scorched and devastated landscape that passed them by as they reached thirty, forty, fifty miles per hour, he kept his head facing forward.

Harrison occupied the front passenger seat. A small touchscreen computer lay on his lap; the screen, cracked and smeared with fingerprints, showed a family portrait. A mother, father, and two adult daughters with their respective partners and their children.

"Don't understand why we gotta babysit these oldies," Harrison complained. He swiped left to move to the next picture. This one was of the mother and father as they stood side by side. A large crack in the screen divided the picture into two. Their files showed that they were in their seventies, and their skin was brown and crinkled, like leather, from too much sun. The man was almost completely bald save for a few strands of light grey hair, bleached by the sun.

"She said we got a duty of care," Brenly repeated. He tried his best to imitate the authority of Walters's voice earlier that day.

"It's punishment, is what it is. She's thrown a wobbly and wants to get rid of us!"

"Just shut up and read the report, will ya?" Brenly snapped.

"All right, all right, keep your shirt on." Harrison threw one of his hands up in defence.

"Let's see…says here the two we're looking for are called Mike and Sylvia Johnson of Brooks Farm. They're in the picture here. They were meant to meet one of their daughters at Sydney Airport last week but never showed up. Daughters tried calling. Neither of them lives local enough to check on 'em. One in Sydney. One in Perth."

"Does it say why they live in the middle of fuckin' nowhere?" Brenly knew that they had at least a further forty minutes' drive ahead of them before they reached their destination. He hoped that their visit wouldn't last long so they could turn around and return to the safety of the city.

Something about the countryside sent a shiver up the back of Brenly's neck.

"The daughter said that they retired out there. He had that, ah…whatcha call it? You know, they found a cure for it? What's it called…old people used to get it all the time? Used to kill them eventually. Used to forget loads—ah yeah, that's it, Alzheimer's. Yeah, he had Alzheimer's disease."

Brenly noticed that Harrison pronounced it "Ult-heimer's."

"They both loved the countryside. The daughter said they hated the fact that they had to move to the city after the War. They were country people born and bred, couldn't wait to get back out here. He popped a few of those AZ things, and they ran off into the bush. Lucky for some, I say. Gotta be real rich to buy yourself some of that AZ now. Got more money than sense, I reckon, or real good health insurance. Bet they live in a palace."

Forty minutes later, Brenly pulled up a dusty driveway outside a modest-sized bungalow. A faded sign at the entrance to the track read "The Johnsons," but the sign needn't have been there. This house was the only one for miles.

They jumped out of the car and listened carefully, but the house was silent. Not even the low buzz of the enormous solar panels on the roof could be heard. The air was dry and hot, and the slight breeze covered Brenly and his colleague in a light red dust. Brenly's eyes felt gritty and his throat sore. He couldn't wait to get back into the air-conditioned car already.

There was only one window this side of the house, but the pane was pitch black, and neither officer could see inside. Brenly looked over to Harrison, and a silent agreement passed between them.

"Looks pretty dead," Harrison suggested. "We sure they didn't just run away someplace else? I'd go nuts out here. Maybe they did too."

"Let's just take a look, and then we can get outta here," Brenly replied.

He walked up the steps to the porch, and Harrison followed him. Their shoes left prints in the thick layer of red dust that covered the wooden boards of the porch. A meshed panel with a spring-loaded hinge covered the front door. He pulled that open first and gave the door a little nudge with his foot. It rested tight against the doorjamb. He tested the handle, and it moved easily in his palm. It wasn't locked. He knocked with three large raps.

"Mr Johnson?" he called out. "Mrs Johnson, you there?" Brenly looked over at his partner, who shrugged in response.

"Let's go in," Harrison suggested. He pushed past Brenly and let himself into the house without a moment's hesitation. As soon as the door swung back on its hinges, they were hit with a stench so strong it almost winded them. Harrison clutched at his nose and mouth, and Brenly retched in the direction of the porch.

From inside the house, they noticed a soft, persistent scratching noise and the low buzz of several insects.

"Come on," Brenly encouraged, and he stepped across the threshold into a lounge area. He copied Harrison and covered his lower face with his hand. His baton remained in the holster of his utility belt.

He spotted the window that they had looked through from the outside, and he retched again when he realised why the pane had appeared so dark. A swarm of fat black flies were covering it from frame to frame. He could see them move now, the blackness alive.

Brenly instructed Harrison to split from him, and he headed in the direction of the kitchen. Harrison went towards what he assumed was the only bedroom. The scratching that they had heard on entry to the house became louder as Brenly got closer to the kitchen door. The door already ajar, he pushed it open with his foot, releasing a second wave of that rank smell. It filled his nostrils with rotting flesh, and he dry-heaved into his hand.

A small square table was positioned in the centre of the kitchen; an overturned chair lay on the floor on one side, and a second remained tucked under the table neatly. Very few kitchen cabinets lined the walls, but all of the doors had been slung open. Some hinges were warped with damage. There was a door to his left that would most likely lead to a pantry.

He didn't open it.

That scratching noise was even clearer now, and he looked around to see where it was coming from. The noise was familiar; it sounded like a dog's clipped claws tapping on a wooden floor. The thought made him glance down, and he noticed that the wooden boards beneath his feet were stained with patches of dark red. A few more steps and the scratching became clearer. This time it was joined by a low, rasping noise, like the breaths of a dying animal.

"Mr Johnson?" he called out, his voice not nearly as confident as when they first arrived at the scene. Across the house, he heard Harrison echo his call.

The kitchen door slammed shut behind him, and Brenly's heart leapt out of his chest. He clutched at it and took deep and steady breaths. He was about to glance back at the door to reassure himself further when something at the bottom of his eyesight caught his attention. There was something—or someone—under the table.

He took one more deep breath and lowered himself so he could check under the table. As he drew level with the underside, he came eye to eye with a pair of piercing blue irises set into a grey face, a rotting face and a human face, or what was left of it. The rasping breaths he had heard a moment ago were rattling out of this...*thing's* mouth.

His eyes travelled down to where that scratching noise had been coming from, as it was even louder now. His heart stopped. The creature's nails were scraping uselessly against the floorboards. In fact, they weren't even nails. The thing had been scratching for so long that all the flesh had been torn away, revealing the bones of its fingertips.

A high scream came from across the house, and Brenly jumped. *Harrison,* he thought. The blue eyes registered the noise and flicked towards the door before returning to Brenly. A growl deep within the creature's chest filled the room, a croaking rumble escaping from within that rotten mouth. Brenly had just enough time to throw himself back against the kitchen floor before the creature launched itself towards him.

Whatever it was, it was too weak to pin him down, and he managed to kick it off and away from him in two clean strikes. A stabbing pain in his ankle on the first attempt jarred his leg midkick, so he swung in again. He shook the pain off, leapt to his feet, and yanked open the kitchen door. He let it swing all the way back on its hinges, not daring to turn back or shut it behind him. He ran towards the room from which Harrison's screams had come.

When he arrived at the bedroom that Harrison had been searching, he was met with a murder scene. The walls were covered in a brown mass of dried blood, just like the kitchen floorboards. A male figure, who Brenly assumed to be Mike Johnson, was on his feet staggering towards Harrison, blood smeared around his rotting face. Chunks of decaying flesh were caught between his teeth. Harrison was on the floor, his face pale and his mouth gaping with shock.

Brenly launched himself forward and dragged Harrison back across the threshold of the bedroom. He hauled Harrison to his feet and slammed the bedroom door behind him.

Without a word, they sprinted back to their waiting squad car. The meshed front door cover banged behind them on its spring.

"What the fuck was that?" Harrison panted. He was crying, gasping for breath between his tears.

"I don't fucking know," Brenly replied. His voice shook as he slammed his foot on the accelerator and sped away from the house. Red smoke bloomed from the car's tyres.

"They were fucking…I don't know…were they even…" Harrison stuttered.

"I don't fuckin' know, but whatever they were, that wasn't human," Brenly shot back.

But Harrison wasn't listening.

Harrison had his left arm resting down the side of his seat away from Brenly. His wrist turned downwards, he was examining his arm, trying not to let Brenly see. There was a large tear in his shirt, and blood seeped through it. He gently folded back his sleeve, and his right hand shook as he did it. Under the blue cuff of his shirt, a chunk of flesh was missing in the two crescent shapes of a set of jaws. A flap of his black skin was hanging from his wrist, but the blood that had been pouring from it only moments ago had already started to congeal. He rolled his sleeve back down and applied pressure to the laceration, concealing a wince.

"Let's get back to the station. Walters can deal with this shit," he hissed through the pain of his arm. Hot, fat tears still rolled down his face.

But on the driver's side of the car, Brenly wasn't listening, either. He was trying to look at his right ankle in the footwell as it pressed on the accelerator. Blood had seeped into the material of his trouser leg, and it poured farther down into his shoe, so his sock squelched. He gave his ankle a light prod with his finger, trying hard to keep the steering wheel level as he almost shrieked in pain.

He gently pulled up the leg of his trousers. A bloody gaping wound the shape of two crescents glowed on his skin. The faint smell of rotting flesh met his nostrils, and he recoiled in disgust.

He let the material fall back down his leg and pushed his foot through the pain and harder onto the throttle, driving back towards the city limits.

Chapter 13

April 2035
Dublin, Northern Ireland

On the third attempt, Janet turned out the lights in the common room and slunk back to the office. She had checked the lock on each window in there twice and then a final and third time before she felt that the room was secure. In her office, she slumped into her chair and shut her eyes. She hated night shifts with a passion, but everyone had to do them at some point, and her turn had come around again. It had come around too quickly for her liking.

But it wasn't so bad on nights when Janet really considered it. Especially on nights like this when all the residents were asleep. Not that they were much bother when they were awake either, to be honest. And on some nights, she could even have a rest herself.

Although tonight she couldn't relax just yet. She sat in the swivel chair, chewing on her thumbnail. Mel had been gone for almost an hour, which meant she should have been back by now.

But was there any real reason to worry? This kind of stuff happened all the time; employees stepping out for a few minutes, leaving only one person in charge. But Janet was utterly convinced that a manager was going to drop in unannounced at any moment. For the first half hour, her eyes had been glued to the window, looking for the telltale beam of headlights.

She started up the television on the desk next to her. She drummed her fingers on the desk as she flicked through the channels, looking for something to distract her for the next half hour or so. Finally she settled on a rerun of *The March Show*. The information panel told Janet that this particular edition was only shown a week ago. Michelle had invited three people onto her show to discuss the success of AZ.

On the screen, the camera cut to each guest as they were introduced, but Janet only recognised Mona Strauss, that awful politician with her squeaky clean smile. Ugh. A plain-faced girl who called herself Jana Duke—probably a fake name, Janet thought—looked sweaty and nervous in front of the camera.

A high-pitched beep came from the switchboard on the wall above the desk. The chilling sound indicated that one of her patients was flatlining. She leapt up and consulted the board—Mrs King in room 23. Janet's stomach plummeted. She grabbed her handheld computer from the desk and sprinted in the direction of the stairs. As she ran, she reminded herself of the steps to resuscitate a patient. *Chest compressions, breaths…one…two…three.*

When she was halfway up the stairs, the noise from the switchboard ended abruptly. The lack of sound made the air eerily quiet.

It would just be her luck that somebody would die on her frickin' watch. It couldn't happen when Mel was there. Oh no, of course not! It had to be when she was by herself, breaking the rule. And what business did that Mrs King even have dying in a place like this, for goodness sake? Why did the old busybody have to go and make herself ill in a rehab centre of all places? And right before her due date too?

Mrs King had been a resident at the Morley Rehabilitation Centre for Alzheimer's Outpatients for almost seven years. She was to be given back to her family next week after a full recovery. That was the plan, until she had fallen into a coma two days ago and hadn't woken up. It seemed desperately sad to Janet that Mrs King would suddenly die when she was so close to going home. And it seemed desperately ironic and completely inconvenient that Mrs King should choose to die when Janet was by herself.

As she ran upstairs, Janet dreaded the sight she would encounter; all manner of scenarios flooded her brain. She would have to wait until Melissa came back, and then she'd have to call management, and she didn't like speaking to them. She'd have to inform Mrs King's family. People would wonder why she had died; people who are cured of Alzheimer's don't just drop dead a week before their due date, for goodness sake.

Goodness, people would blame her. People would think she had something to do with it. She might lose her job.

Her heart thudded with nerves. She burst into Mrs King's room with her eyes screwed tightly shut. She pictured Mrs King's flailing body caught up in her white bed sheets as she twitched from another fit. Mrs King's body on the floor in a vast pool of blood that Janet would have to clean up. Mrs King's skull cracked open from falling out of bed…

Finally, she opened her eyes. There was Mrs King, as she expected, but she was lying still in her single bed. Attached to her index finger was the device that monitored her earlier failing heart rate. From across the room, Janet could see Mrs King's chest rise and fall gently. She appeared to be completely fine after all.

I should check her, though. I really ought to check her…

Janet's head began to buzz again. She moved closer to the bed and felt Mrs King's pulse. The rhythm was erratic. Out of her eyesight, Mrs King's nostrils flared.

Janet observed the pallor of Mrs King's skin. In the weeks leading up to the coma, it had gone an unusual light grey colour. The doctor had advised Janet that this was fairly common in AZ patients and that it wasn't anything to worry about. Janet had believed him.

She also believed him when he said that Mrs King would wake up soon.

Janet bent over her patient's prone body to fiddle with the instrument measuring her pulse. There must have been something wrong with this bastarding thing. Bloody machines. They had a mind of their own, couldn't be trusted. She groaned with frustration and rearranged the device.

With her head tilted away, she did not notice Mrs King's eyes snap open or see Mrs King's lips pull back over her teeth in a snarl.

She did, however, catch the scent of rotting flesh, and she wrinkled her nose in disgust. She pulled away, attempting to stand up straight and put more space between her and that filthy stench.

As Janet pushed back from the bed, Mrs King sunk her bared teeth into the exposed flesh of Janet's neck.

The kill was so instantaneous that Janet did not emit a sound as the weight of her body tore itself free from the section of neck between Mrs King's lips. Her legs collapsed beneath her, and her body crumpled to the floor.

As she died, she did not think of her family or of Mrs King's visiting relatives tomorrow but of Mel and of the TV still rolling downstairs and how much trouble they would both be in the next morning when their manager arrived to a swimming pool of blood and a cannibalistic patient.

I arrived home with my family late that afternoon, heavy with the kind of exhaustion you only get from sitting in the sun all day. The weather had been too good for us to pass up, and so we had packed a picnic earlier that day and set off for the nearest park.

We had spent the day laughing and talking, reminiscing about times before I had fallen ill. By the time the clouds had begun to roll in and we decided to head back home, all three of us were grinning from ear to ear.

And the best part of the entire day? I felt like Lois and I had fallen in love all over again. She loved me; I could tell that by the way she sneaked heart-eyed glances at me from her side of the car. And how she reached across to take my hand as we cruised along.

When I got home, I unloaded the empty boxes of Tupperware into the sink, ready to wash up. I looked out on our back garden; it was alive with vibrant pinks and whites, the fallen blossoms covering the grass like a blanket of snow. The garden had been severely neglected, and I considered working out there tomorrow, but not now. The day we had had was finally catching up to me because my head was starting to feel fuzzy.

Recently, by the late afternoon, a dull ache would start encroaching on the back of my brain. The feeling was enough to exhaust me, and the pain was too distracting to attempt to get anything done.

"You OK, Mum?" Jessie asked, concern in her voice as I turned to look at her. I could feel my eyelids beginning to droop.

"Yeah…I'm just a bit…tired. I guess…I'll be all right in a minute," I mumbled back. I felt as if somebody was pushing down hard on the base of my skull. Jessie wasn't convinced.

She took my arm and started to manoeuvre me into the living room and towards the couch.

The television was on already, the news playing on repeat in the background. Jessie went to turn it off before I waved a feeble arm to stop her.

"No, don't. Just leave it on for a minute," I muttered as I lowered myself into the thick folds of the sofa.

"OK. Let me know if you need anything, Mum. Have a little sleep," she suggested. She went over to the window and shut the curtains tight, plunging the room into semi-darkness; it was lit only by the television now. She shut the door softly behind her.

I closed my eyes and tried to will the pain in my head away. I pictured scenes from earlier that day and told myself that the pain in my head was worth it for how perfect our morning and early afternoon had been. I was so lucky to be able to share this time with my family again and to be healthy. It was something that so many people took for granted, but I knew I never would again. These hours and minutes spent with Jessie and Lois were even more important to me now that I knew what it was like to have no time at all.

I called out to the television, and the news anchors' conversation decreased in volume. The low murmur of voices that came from the speaker comforted me, and within minutes, I felt myself drifting into the realm of sleep, warmed by the idea that Lois and I were back on track.

Unconsciousness crept in, giving me slight relief from the heavy pressure at the back of my head.

As I slept, the news anchor continued to speak. A photograph of a care home just outside Dublin flashed on the screen, the name of it too small to read. Yellow police tape was slung around the perimeter, drooping off the surrounding trees. If you looked closely at the old Victorian building, you could see the front door hanging off its hinges and the remains of a smashed window in the grass.

Uneven footsteps made in blood travelled down the steps of the huge house. A caption for the image scrolled across the ticker at the bottom of the screen: *BREAKING NEWS: Massacre in Dublin nursing home. Dozens dead, many in hospital. Several more missing. Attacker still at large.*

The screen split in two. On one side, the news anchor remained in the studio staring intensely into the camera. On the other side, a reporter stood outside the nursing home.

The reporter pointed to the bloody footprints that led from the door of the home, across the grass, and into the woodland surrounding it. He then indicated several ambulances behind him. Their back doors were wide open, admitting wheeled gurneys heavy with bodies.

The ambulances prepared to depart, though they would not make it to their destination.

I slept soundly, yet the ache in the back of my head raged on.

Chapter 14

April 2035
Dublin, Ireland

Casey suddenly found herself awake. Something had roused her from sleep, but she wasn't sure what. She turned onto her side and looked at her phone: five thirty in the morning. And there it was, that noise again. The noise that had woken her up. Through the delirium of sleep, she tried to listen carefully.

Somebody was going through their bin. She heard the plastic lid smacking against the body of it and the sound of paper and plastic being tossed around. Small thuds as something heavy hit the grass.

"Babe, can you scare that animal off? Tell it to quit making so much noise," she mumbled to his silhouetted back, her voice still thick with sleep.

"You do it," he muttered back. She prodded him hard in the base of his spine, and he let out a grunt. The poke was enough, and he pulled himself slowly from their bed and staggered over to the window. He pulled back the curtain to check on the commotion in the garden but let out another grunt of dissatisfaction. The morning was still too dark to see anything.

"Make me breakfast while you're up," she added as he pulled on his thick woollen dressing gown. He let out a final grunt in reply and shuffled downstairs.

Casey pressed her pillow tight against her ears to drown out the noise from outside. Through the muffled protection of the material, she heard the front door open and then there was silence.

An hour later, she woke up with a jolt at the sound of her alarm screeching at her. She threw her arm out to push her boyfriend out of bed again. He needed extra encouragement to wake up on Mondays. Her hand met the cold, empty air where his body should have been.

He must be downstairs, she thought to herself. She listened out for noises in another part of the house. Somebody was moving about in the kitchen; heavy footsteps thudded across the linoleum. He must be making her breakfast after all. Her stomach threatened a growl at the thought of bacon sandwiches.

She slid out from under the duvet and into her dressing gown that hung on the back of the bedroom door. *Hopefully he's put the kettle on. I could do with a coffee,* her half-asleep brain grumbled.

She was hit with a blast of cold air when she came out of her bedroom. She wrapped her dressing gown around her a little tighter and crossed the hall to poke her head into her daughter's room. She was already wide awake, sitting upright on her bed, reading a thick book. Dark rims of eyeliner framed her eyes.

"Breakfast?" Casey called.

Her daughter nodded in response, but her closely cropped jet-black hair didn't flinch at the movement of her head. "I'll be down in a minute," she replied.

Casey nodded and retreated out of the room. She headed towards the stairs and took them carefully, her limbs still dull from sleep.

She stifled a yawn as she reached the bottom stair but allowed her body to pull itself into a stretch. Her neck and back clicked in relief. *Another awful night's sleep on that crappy mattress,* her muscles whined. They had meant to buy a new one at the weekend, but time had gotten away from them, which meant their shopping plans had to be scrapped.

Casey could still hear Mason in the kitchen. And despite the fact that he must have been down there for at least an hour, his footsteps were still slow and sleepy. She couldn't hear the sound of the kettle being boiled or any bacon sizzling away in a frying pan on the stove. Her stomach let out a hollow moan of disappointment.

That cold draught caught the back of her neck, and she heard the creak of a door on its hinges. She spun around to find the front door wide open. She made a performance of stomping over to shut it, making sure that her loud footsteps would be heard from the kitchen. She hoped that Mason might hear her and apologise for leaving the door open in the middle of a freezing April morning. What a complete idiot.

As she approached the door, she recalled the events earlier that morning. Something had been outside; somebody had been rummaging through her bin. She looked over to the beat-up shelter where the bin normally rested and silently fumed to herself. The bin was upturned, and trash was strewn all over the lawn. She seethed as she set it back upright and collected the fallen rubbish. She slammed the lid back down and stamped into the house, ready for a screaming match with Mason.

On her way back into the house, she shoved the front door so hard behind her that it rebounded off its frame and swung back open.

On her approach to the kitchen, something caught her eye on the floor in front of her, and she looked down. Muddy footprints stained the cream carpet. The footprints were a mess; Mason had staggered into the house with bare feet. The prints started from the muddy patch of grass out the front and then trailed into the house, circling around the hallway. One print lay on the bottom step of the stairs but did not go any farther. The rest of them went in the direction of the kitchen, where Mason was.

Casey followed the prints, marching down the hallway and towards the kitchen. Mason had stopped moving about in there; perhaps he nervously awaited her reaction to the mud lining her carpet. *Well, he is definitely going to get a reaction now. No breakfast, didn't even bother to pick up any of that mess outside,* and *he walked his muddy-ass feet all over my fucking floor.* Red mist clouded over Casey's vision as she threw open the kitchen door. Her mouth was a horrible, jagged scar on her face, her forehead creased into a harsh frown.

But the sight of Mason caught her short. He was not looking at her; he was not even facing her, but she knew immediately that something was wrong. Perhaps she should have known it sooner when she found the garden and the hallway in such a mess.

The dressing gown he had pulled on earlier was covered in mud, the left sleeve torn shorter than usual, and...

Her eyes travelled down his left arm where it still hung uselessly at his side, the little stub of his elbow pointing downwards, the forearm and hand missing- but that was not what was unusual, for Mason had lost his lower arm and hand years before.

What was unusual was that at the end of his right arm, his fingers were held in a claw shape, and the palm of his hand had turned an ashen grey colour. Well, what Casey could see of his palm; his hand was covered in so much blood that she could barely tell that the backs of them were meant to be dark brown.

Her eyes moved from his hand to the back of his head. His hair sat in neat braids across his scalp; they dangled low across his broad shoulders. His body quivered, but his head stayed completely still like it was trying to pick up a distant noise or smell. *Was* he trying to sniff something? She could hear air passing through his nostrils as he inhaled. And his breath...He wasn't breathing right. He sounded odd. His breathing was loud and laboured, uneven.

A small croak escaped his mouth.

She took a step back, standing on something behind her, a foot. She leapt into the air and spun around. Her daughter, Meredith, winced in pain and shot her mother a furious look. She opened her mouth to hiss an insult when she caught sight of Mason behind Casey. Her eyes darted from the back of his head to his gnarled and bloodied hand down by his side to the muddy footprints he had made across the floor.

Meredith's mouth remained open in a silent O, and Casey watched as her daughter's chest rose in a sharp intake of breath. She knew what was coming so she slapped her hand over her daughter's mouth immediately and dragged her back through the kitchen doorway and into the hall.

"What the—" Meredith began, her speech still muffled under Casey's hand.

"Shhh," Casey hissed.

Panic had begun to course through her veins. *What the fuck indeed. What the fuck happened to Mason?* she thought. *What the fuck happened earlier when he went outside? Who the fuck was out there?* Realisation dawned on Casey like an ocean wave, cold and heavy. Another question had sprung into her mind-

And it was answered almost immediately by Meredith's face. Her daughter's eyes, so wide they were almost popping out of her skull, were fixed on something just over Casey's shoulder.

Chapter 15

April 2035
An extract taken from an international online newspaper called InterNewsOnline:

UNKNOWN VIRUS KILLS HUNDREDS IN IRELAND. EXPERTS SAY IT IS UNLIKELY TO CROSS THE IRISH SEA.
By Jodie Fisher **Tuesday 17 April 2035**

Experts say that a deadly virus that has claimed the lives of 916 people and is spreading through Ireland is unlikely to cross the Irish Sea to neighbours Wales, Scotland, and England. These claims follow a statement from the World Health Organisation (WHO) that admit they have no idea where the virus has come from.

The disease, which has not yet been given a name, appeared in Ireland in the last fortnight, but experts say it is still too soon to specify how the virus is transmitted, and they have been unable to identify patient 0. Evidence suggests that the virus is not airborne, which makes it difficult for it to cross sea borders.

The UK government is advising anybody who was expecting to travel to Ireland in the next month to cancel their plans until the virus is contained. Later today, parliament is expected to discuss whether UK borders should remain open.

⁂

Jack was starting to feel travel-sick. At least he thought it was travel sickness, though he hadn't felt well since he woke up that morning. He had woken in a cold sweat, his head pounding and his stomach churning. Of all the days in the year to get sick, why did it have to be today?

He rummaged in the pocket of the seat in front of him and found what he was looking for, a paper bag. His neighbouring passenger watched him out of the corner of her eye, her nose crinkled in disgust. She swivelled in her seat away from him, intent on looking out of the window to watch the clouds drift by.

It had all started yesterday, he thought to himself. He had finished work early and had meant to go straight home but instead headed to the pub to meet his friends for a few beers. It was only meant to be a couple, as he had needed to pack for his flight from Dublin to Edinburgh the next day, but time had escaped him, and he found himself leaving the pub at closing time. His suitcase waited at home, still empty.

He had opted to walk home, as the weather was beginning to take a turn towards summer. The night air had been fresh; he needn't have worn his suit jacket. He had almost been at his doorstep when he blacked out, and when he woke up again, the sky had taken on a pink glow.

That wasn't what was unusual. Jack was often stumbling home, drunk, after breaking his one-drink rule. But as he had stood, he had felt a soreness in his left ankle.

At the time, he assumed that he must have hit it on something as he went down. He didn't bother to check his foot until the cab ride to the airport, and now it was probably infected. When he had rolled down his sock, he had found a small hole, no bigger than a two-euro piece. The laceration itself was shallow, but wow, it sure did hurt, and it was bright red with infection. A little puss had leaked out. He had raided the Boots in the departures lounge and slapped some antiseptic on it and swathed it in a bandage. He vowed if he had time, then he would visit a doctor during his trip.

And now here he was. His ankle was inflamed, and he was overcome with nausea. He told himself that he would find a hospital or a doctor as soon as he landed. Get prescribed with some antibiotics and then be on his way to the meeting scheduled at 3:00 p.m. That was if he found the time, of course. It wouldn't hurt to wait a little bit longer. Maybe he could wait until tomorrow to get seen. What was the worst that could happen?

It wasn't out of character for Jack to completely ignore his ailments. Once when he broke his arm, he went so long without visiting a hospital that by the time he saw a doctor, the bone had already started to heal itself. It had to be rebroken and reset. Another time when he cracked a tooth on an olive stone, he avoided the dentist until a giant abscess formed on his upper gum and made him look half chipmunk.

Could the cut on his leg be any worse than all the other scrapes and bumps he had had in his life? Probably not. Visiting the hospital might delay him. And it would be frightfully unprofessional to arrive to his meeting late.

It would be even more frightfully unprofessional not to arrive at all.

Part Three

Chapter 16

May 2035

All three of us jerked our heads upwards at the TV; it had come on suddenly without being instructed. At the top of the screen, "BREAKING NEWS" read in huge white lettering across a red background. A newscaster stared intently into the screen; she was waiting for something, sitting behind a desk in the studio.

Below her on a ticker were the words "World Health Organisation claims that AZ drug is to blame for virus… Government orders the interruption of all television to bring you the latest update…"

"What the—" Jessie began. She put down her moving piece of the board game we had been playing.

"Good evening. I'm Alma Hill," the newscaster said as she pushed back a strand of thick black hair from her eyes. "Earlier today, leading experts at the World Health

Organisation announced new information about the virus that is devastating Western parts of the world.

"Experts believe that the virus began following a mutation of the Alzheimer's treatment AZ. AZ, which was first released to the general public in 2032, was praised for its ability to cure long-suffering Alzheimer's patients. Human trials were conducted in the United and Reformed States of America previous to the drug's release, but it was thought that there were no long-term side effects…"

My heart stopped. And although my eyes and ears were trained on the television screen, my other senses were elsewhere, scouting the room. I had the strongest impression that I was being watched. I could sense rather than see that my daughter's eyes were already flicking between the television and where I sat.

"At least sixteen million people worldwide are said to have used the AZ drug in a bid to reverse the side effects of the debilitating Alzheimer's disease. Short-term symptoms of the drug included headaches and migraines, increased hunger, and a greyish pallor to skin tone. However, family members began to report fitting, convulsions, and aggressive behaviour. It is believed that these symptoms were actually early signs of the virus…

"Following the discovery by the World Health Organisation, the government announced plans to close the UK borders. The government had previously been accused of complacency as the disease grew in notoriety. We go to our correspondent, Jill Evans, who is outside the Houses of Parliament right now. Jill, what can you tell us?"

The screen cut in half horizontally. On one side, Alma Hill stayed in the studio; on the other side, the aforementioned Jill Evans was poised outside parliament. She held an umbrella in one hand and her notes in the other, a microphone above her head just out of the camera's view.

"Hi, Alma. Well, the government has announced that UK borders will be closed effective immediately. They are also asking anybody who has taken the drug to please hand themselves into police custody as soon as possible. Alternatively, if you know of anybody who has taken AZ, please contact the police using the new emergency number rolling across your screens right now. The government and police say it is vital that all patients are taken into quarantine as soon as possible to prevent the infection from spreading further."

"And what's the atmosphere like in London, Jill?" Alma asked.

"Alma, as you can probably guess, tensions are running pretty high now. A large gathering of people has formed on the grass outside the building behind me. When I was speaking to people a moment ago, some of them claimed that the government has known about the virus far longer than they are letting on."

"There is evidence of that, though, isn't there, Jill?"

"Yes, there is. There are reports as far back as January, when a grandmother attacked her granddaughter in Georgia of the URSA. The grandmother was in fact an ex-Alzheimer's patient who had been in the trials for AZ. She is thought to be one of the first people to be affected by the virus. However, it's quite difficult to tell at this early stage."

"Can you tell us why it took so long for that story to break?"

"Yes, Alma. URSA authorities say that the incident was not reported to them for a period of eight weeks—"

"Eight weeks!" Alma exclaimed.

"Yes, that's right. It is not known how the police eventually found out about it—"

The television switched off just as abruptly as it had come on. I had been so glued to it that I hadn't noticed Lois get up and switch it off at the socket. Without a word, she returned to her seat, but she did not take her eyes off me.

I felt Jessie moving next to me. She had pulled out her phone and had begun to dial a number onto the screen. Her thumb hovered over the call option, summoning the police at any moment. All she would need to do is let the phone ring once, and her location would be tracked instantly.

In one fluid movement, Lois reached across and snatched the phone from Jessie's grasp. Lois's grip was soft but had the authority of a well-practiced parent, like a mother confiscating an obnoxiously loud toy from a toddler. She gave a small shake of the head at Jessie's confused expression and turned the phone off completely. She settled it on the armrest next to her, out of Jessie's reach.

Lois and I locked eyes, and she reached for my hand. She grasped it tightly as she watched my face. Between us passed a silent agreement, witnessed only by Jessie. The police would not come, at least not today.

Chapter 17

May 2035

Michelle struggled to maintain concentration as a small crowd began to surge behind her. It had been a while since she had corresponded live, she thought, and it wasn't as easy as it used to be. Or maybe she was just getting too old for it. Either way, despite her initial excitement, now she prayed for the time to go faster so she could finish the bottle of scotch she had stowed away in her overnight bag.

Once, a long time ago, she had lived for the exhilaration that live reporting gave her. The buzz that couldn't be produced in the studio had been like a drug. It was a huge adrenaline rush to be live on TV while her safety was at risk; her reactions and surroundings were uncensored and unrehearsed. Now she was used to the comfort of the studio, which was only a few minutes' car ride from her North London house. She had earned that, she assured herself. She had put in all of the hard work while she was young and built on it to reach this point.

Now she was allowed to sit back and watch the new generation falter midsentence as bombs shook the ground beneath them and debris threatened to lodge itself in their unprotected skin. And she could watch it all from the comfort of her own home and with a bottle of Chardonnay.

Not that there were many bombs going off anymore. The world was in relative peace and had been since the Australian Civil War had ended. But it would only be a matter of time before tension grew again somewhere in some remote part of the world. With so many differing views and religions on this planet, there was bound to be a clash sooner or later.

"We're on live in sixty seconds, Michelle." Her producer waved at her and then indicated the camera. The camerawoman fiddled with the buttons on the side of the camera to focus on Michelle's face in preparation for the broadcast.

A week earlier, Elsa, her producer, had broken the news that Michelle's late-night talk show was no longer receiving the same ratings it had once had. Viewer figures were plummeting too. This information was soon followed up with a plan, and it involved riding the wave of fear about the latest deadly disease that was gripping the world. Michelle was to report live from a recently infected area in a bid to increase the public's interest once more, and Elsa had said the plan was foolproof. In conducting this particular report, they could make up for any of the past misgivings, and the country would fall back in love with Michelle's heroic and hands-on attitude.

Initially, when the suggestion first came up, Michelle had hesitated. If she followed through with this, then it would break her part of the deal she had with Medipharm. After a while, she convinced herself that saving her career was far more important than saving the careers of those from whom she had accepted the bribe. She decided to go ahead with the report, and if Medipharm got in touch, well…so be it. *Just let them try and take the money back from me, now that I've already fucking spent it.*

Tonight they were in Edinburgh, not normally considered an area of danger, but it was where the latest outbreak had been recorded. *Although it could scarcely be called an outbreak,* Michelle thought. All the patients had been contained and quarantined within hours, a small enough amount that it had taken only an infinitesimal squad of police and one secure ward to hold them back and sedate them. The virus was slow in engulfing the map of the United Kingdom. Edinburgh might have been the next city it took, but it wasn't likely.

The British know how to organise a retaliation. Not like those insufferable Americans, Michelle thought as she pushed a few stray strands of her blond hair off her face. Appallingly, they seemed to have given up already. One tiny outbreak in Georgia, and all of a sudden, they had screamed, "Pandemic! Pandemic!" instead of stopping the virus in its tracks before it began to spread. *The virus can't be that bad—the English stopped it easily enough,* Michelle thought pointedly.

Michelle adjusted her suit jacket. The day had been uncharacteristically hot and humid for Scottish weather. Sweat was beginning to build up on the back of Michelle's neck, and she felt an uncomfortable clamminess beneath the cotton of her blouse.

"And in ten…nine…eight…" Elsa began. Michelle plastered on her best smile and tried to ignore her increasingly sweaty back. In one hand she held her microphone, and in the other she grasped the notes that she had taken earlier that day. "Three…two…one." There was a thumbs-up from Elsa, and a red light on the camera lit up.

"Good evening. I'm Michelle March, and I'm reporting to you live outside the Royal Edinburgh Hospital in Scotland where we have received reports of a fresh outbreak of the deadly virus, AZ. Behind me, you can see a large crowd gathering now; in the crowd are several family and friends of those who have now been quarantined on a single ward inside the hospital. They wait patiently outside for any news of their loved ones, unable to adopt a bedside vigil." She gestured behind her to the baying crowd, penned in by armed police officers.

As Michelle paused for effect, she received another thumbs-up from her producer. She had made a good start. She compared reporting live on location to the skill of riding a bicycle; you never truly forgot how to do it.

"Earlier today, we received exclusive reports that ten new cases of the virus had appeared in Edinburgh. All ten victims are thought to have come into contact with the drug AZ, which gives the recipient rabies-like symptoms. The virus first became apparent earlier this year and has been upgraded from an epidemic in a few major cities to a worldwide pandemic. This is one of the first recorded outbreaks in the United Kingdom since borders were closed earlier this month—"

Michelle heard the unmistakeable sound of three gunshots go off behind her. Her resolve faltered slightly, and she could feel panicked sweat creep up the base of her spine. She struggled to find the trail that she had been following and told herself that this used to happen all the time back in her day. She should be used to gunshots, she reassured herself. Their noise had practically been the soundtrack of her youthful working life. She racked her brain and tried to find the end of the thread to the sentence she had begun.

To the right of her camera, she saw Elsa motion to her to carry on. She flapped her arm frantically, scared that the public would lose interest if they saw Michelle wavering. Michelle reached up to the earpiece in her left ear, and the papers she held clumsily grazed her face as she nodded and pretended to receive a message through her earpiece.

"Um…as you can…as you just heard…there appears to be…er…a slight disturbance behind me. I'm sure there's nothing to fear…the…errr…crowds are getting quite large at the moment, so the police are probably rattling off a few warning shots," Michelle stuttered, relieved when she finally managed to finish her sentence.

Her producer nodded and mouthed, "Good." Michelle knew that Elsa would have liked that line. Elsa was not a huge fan of the police and found that they made a perfect scapegoat at almost every opportunity if a live broadcast wasn't going as anticipated.

Michelle tried her best to continue, but her concentration wavered further as she realised that the camerawoman wasn't even watching her. She was looking over Michelle's shoulder instead, more interested in the commotion that was going on out of Michelle's eyesight. The camera dipped slightly. Outraged, Michelle vowed that the camerawoman wouldn't work on a live transmission ever again. *The audacity,* she thought venomously, *to beg to want to be a part of this and then at the first moment, she's looking away!* Michelle could scarcely believe it and considered putting a stop to the broadcast so she could give the girl a piece of her mind.

Michelle caught herself before she stepped out of the camera's line of sight. She gave herself a discreet shake. Now was not the time. She needed to concentrate on the task at hand; her live feed might be cut if she paused for much longer, and that might mean her career would be dead and buried by the end of the night.

"Police have warned the public not to—"

Michelle knew better than to look; she must remain professional at all times. But now Elsa watched the crowd behind Michelle too. The shouts had begun to get much louder. She moved her head fractionally to catch a glimpse of what was happening. In the moment it took for her to move her head and see something out of the corner of her eye, she realised that the shouts she had been hearing were not shouts. They were moans.

Low, rasping moans…and these moans were joined by animalistic howls. They were layered one on top of the other until they were almost deafening. She could not recall having ever heard such a sound before, but on instinct, her body shivered so fiercely that she could almost feel her bones rattle inside her. The hairs on her neck stood so erect that she could almost feel them piercing tiny holes through the material of her suit.

It was over in seconds.

Michelle was hit with the force of a small car and was thrown to the floor. The camerawoman suffered the same fate. The equipment clattered to the ground, and the direct feed to the studio still ran as it filmed the entire act. Before Michelle had even registered the scene, there was a woman on top of her. She was midsixties with dyed dark hair. She had the slightly wrinkled face of somebody who had laughed enough but had smoked too many cigarettes. There was a faint aroma of tobacco on her skin and her breath.

She was perfectly average, you could contest. Perhaps she had once been a mother or a grandmother. But the fresh bloodstains across her white blouse indicated that now she was something far removed from a family woman. In her initial confusion, Michelle wanted to holler and ask how on earth the woman thought she could get away with leaping on one of the most successful news anchors of all time.

Michelle opened her mouth to protest when the woman on top of her ripped her tongue from her throat. The words she had meant to say died in her chest to be replaced by a guttural scream so loud and shrill it pierced the eardrums of anybody close enough to consider rescuing her.

The woman tore the navy blue jacket from Michelle's shoulders, and Michelle screamed as the woman, who may have once had a kind face, plunged her teeth into Michelle's bare neck. She pulled a chunk of flesh away in the process. Michelle's screams, once clear, were now reduced to a bubbling gurgle barely heard over the snarling and snapping sounds that emitted from the woman on top of her.

The frenzied attacker split Michelle's stomach open as if she had pulled apart a large, juicy orange, presenting all of Michelle's lower internal organs. She ripped out the intestines and shovelled them into her mouth. She devoured them as if it were her first meal in months.

As the assault continued, Michelle considered that this might be the last live show she would ever do. She thought of her family and her cheating husband. She thought of how much of her money he would inherit and how much of it would be spent on his mistresses. Her eyes still open, they stared straight into the camera that still lay abandoned on the floor.

⋏

In the newsroom, several hundred miles away, a producer screamed, *"Cut the feed. Cut the fucking feed."*

But it was too late. Michelle March's death and the brutal execution of her two team members had been broadcast live to twenty-eight million homes across the country and would be online in a matter of minutes.

Part Four

Chapter 18

May 2035

An extract taken from an international online newspaper called InterNewsOnline:

AZ PILL TO BLAME! PUBLIC URGED TO STAY INDOORS AMID FURTHER VIRUS PANIC!

By Jodie Fisher   **Wednesday 23 May 2035**

EXTENDED EXCLUSIVE

It has emerged that the drug AZ is to blame for the new virus that has claimed the lives of millions worldwide. The British government is urging more patients who have used AZ to come forward and admit themselves into quarantine after the World Health Organisation (WHO) upgraded the virus to pandemic status. They are also asking those who have not taken the drug to stay indoors and secure their homes through fears of the infected toll rising. At present, almost a quarter of the world's population are said to have been affected by this latest and most toxic virus.

Earlier this month, Ireland announced that the infected toll had risen above the country's healthy population and suggested that the AZ virus can be transmitted through deadly bites from the infected. The WHO have not been able to successfully detain or test an infected person, so it has not been confirmed that this is the cause of transmission.

Executives at Medipharm Inc., the company responsible for the development and distribution of the drug, are being called into the firing line amid claims that the company knew about the damaging effects of the drug and failed to report them to NICE, the regulatory body responsible for drug production. Further to this, there have been claims that the corporation deliberately prevented the news of the virus being publicised. Evidence has come to light that several key news personalities had been receiving bribes in exchange for their silence.

Professor Saanvi Singh, who was part of the original team that conducted the initial research into the drug and piloted the animal trials, was found dead in her North London home last week. On the drug's release, she was hailed as a worldwide hero and was being considered for a knighthood later this year until news of the virus first broke.

It has been revealed that she had failed to report damning evidence in the animal trial that would have prevented any further development and the eventual sale of the drug.

Evidence found on her home computer, which had been seized during raids early last week, suggest that the mice she tested on had exhibited unhealthy side effects after taking the drug. It has not been suggested that she was responsible for the bribes to news outlets.

Police are not treating her death as suspicious and have ruled out foul play. It is thought that she took her own life in the early hours of Friday 18 May.

Police Force Issued with Guns
Prime Minister Malorie Ford called for calm throughout the country as the infected toll had begun to outnumber the healthy in several countries, including Ireland, Australia, and large parts of Western Europe. She advised that the police force, who last week were given handguns, and the NHS are doing all they can to prevent further infection. Many people have criticised the introduction of guns into the United Kingdom's police force. However, chief constable Natasha Hathaway has defended their use and reassured the public that the guns will not be a permanent fixture in the police's arsenal.

She advised that the guns had been introduced as a means of protecting the force and the public from the imminent threat of violence from those outside quarantine and that this was a decision that was not easily made. Following new temporary laws, every officer will be required to undergo specialised training so they can be issued a three-month-long permit, which will allow them to possess and use the weapon. After the three-month trial period is over, the presence of handguns in the police force and the situation with the virus will be reevaluated.

It has been suggested that the police are adopting a shoot to immobilise policy and enquiries will be made where accidental death has occurred.

The Infected
So far, infected countries span the entire world, with Australia and Ireland seeming to be the most affected at this time. All flights to and from these countries are being cancelled. It is believed that a remote island off the coast of South America is the only location the virus has not affected.

Resistance Attempts
Amongst those who have begun a quarantine resistance to the virus are Japan, Madagascar, and Cuba. It has been suggested that the first country to organise such a resistance was China, who are rumoured to have set up camps throughout their country. However, contact with the Chinese has been limited since the virus began infecting the country, and it is not known how successful China has been in its attempts to separate the sick from the healthy. Experts suggest that the country and its population are both far too vast for any operation to be effective.

To avoid further spread to the United Kingdom, the government had announced that the UK borders would be closed for an unspecified amount of time. It is unclear when Ms Ford will reconsider the reopening of our borders, but she is hopeful that in keeping them closed, spread of infection will be lessened. Ford is confident that the actions the country has taken so far are enough to keep the population safe. In addition to the border closures, she has ordered all public places to be shut, issuing a countrywide state of emergency.

Right-wing critics are suggesting that the quarantined patients still residing in England should be extradited to Ireland in a bid to keep the mainland safe. But Ford has remained hopeful that those in quarantine will be cured soon and that no additional action will need to be taken.

Advice
Citizens are advised to secure all windows and doors, avoid all further contact with those suspected of harbouring the virus, and remain inside until further instructions are made clear. The police are also advising people that if they have any further questions, they should call the emergency hotline number as advertised. Under no circumstances should the infected be approached. All infected persons are considered to be highly dangerous.

I gingerly removed the holster I strapped around my chest and gently placed it onto the seat next to me. Any apprehensions I had about using the gun had drifted away after I received the permit. At first, like the other members of my team, it had repulsed and scared me, but now I felt mildly empowered. However, I was still unsure about the necessity of it.

In my mind, the use of guns would only ever cause more violence. In the hands of human beings, they could become misused or stolen.

I wasn't keen on taking the gun home with me, either. I would have preferred to leave it in the safety of my locker at work, but that was just asking for it to be nicked. I had been instructed to take it home, but when it was there, it felt like a burden to me. Even out of sight, I could feel its presence in the house, like a huge black shadow looming over my shoulder.

At first I kept it a secret, something we were instructed to do. The general public weren't meant to know that their country's police force would carry their own versions of the same GLOCKs that the URSA law enforcement had once abolished from their weaponry. The UK government had promised to make the announcement when the time came, but it had leaked to the press, and the online news channels had inserted it into every single AZ-related story they could.

I started the engine of the SUV with the push of a button. The car shuddered as it came to life, and its headlights lit up automatically as it started. I pulled slowly out of my parking space and navigated the car park until I reached the main road. My late-night shift had been a quiet one with very few calls. I had spent most of the night wondering why I had to work at all. But the chief had threatened us with disciplinary action if anybody failed to turn up. We all had a duty to protect the public, and our protection was even more important than ever now, according to him.

As I had meandered through the streets in my squad car earlier that evening, I had assumed that people must have actually followed the government's advice and were staying inside to avoid infection. It was a rare occasion when the public actually listened to the instructions they were given, but they must have been spooked. Even we were spooked.

I considered Reece and how she had not declared herself yet. It was a dangerous game, avoiding our responsibility. It was no secret that she had once had Alzheimer's; all our friends knew, and our neighbours were sure to have realised. And it was no secret that she had been cured of the disease, either. My only relief was that I had always been a private person when I was at work. Apart from my boss, I was very reluctant to tell the people I worked with anything about my personal life. And that habit appeared to have paid off.

But in the back of my mind, I knew we weren't safe, and I wasn't sure how much longer we could pretend that Reece would be OK. Now that we had her back, of sound mind and sound health, I was reluctant to give her up again. I had already discovered what my life was like without her, and it had been hell. I wasn't ready to go through that a second time.

As I followed my usual route home, I thought harder about the use of a gun. I had mastered the training and received my permit almost immediately. I leaned over to the glove compartment and pulled it out. It was a small piece of plastic, no bigger than a credit card. It had my name and signature on one side, and on the other was the same emblem that appeared on the front of a British passport. It declared the holder of the permit was able to possess and use a GLOCK PRINT 90. The permit would last for three months before being considered for renewal.

I replaced the card in the glove box and felt for the pistol in its holder. The weapon itself was stainless steel, the grip made from toughened glass, which made it easier to scan the palm and fingerprints of the holder. The pistol was cool to the touch under my fingers, and my stomach flipped at the idea of using it outside training.

A bright light source half a mile ahead distracted me from the gun in my hand, and I dropped it back onto the seat. I slowed the car as I approached a small cottage to the left of the road. It was one of those houses that you only notice when you're a passenger. When you're behind the wheel, you're always going too fast and concentrating too much to see anything. I stopped the car on the edge of the gravelled driveway and looked out the passenger side window.

The house was ablaze with electricity; it seemed like every single light was on in there, but I knew straight away that nobody was home. The front door was wide open, and only one car sat in the driveway. I considered getting out of my car, but was it worth it? If it were just an empty house, then I would spook myself for nothing. I scanned the surrounding area. Nothing else was amiss. No windows had been smashed, so it was probably not a breaking and entering incident, and the car was untouched. I stopped. There was something up ahead, moving around in the middle of the road.

I put the car into gear and cruised slowly forward, pulling away from the house. I squinted slightly to make out what I had seen. It was a humanlike shape, but it was hunched over and had its back to me. I could work out the top of its head, torso, and limbs in the half-light of my headlamps. I flicked them onto full beam. At the sudden burst of light, the creature tossed its head over its shoulder and glared at me momentarily. It was an IC1 male, about seventy years old from the look of his grey hair. He was naked from the waist up. He was unnaturally fast for his presumed age, and he pressed farther down the road. His unnatural speed meant he ran awkwardly on tired and old legs away from my approaching car.

I was about to wind down my window as I got close and considered calling out to him when he stopped suddenly. His head snapped back to me and he let out a low growl of anger. I took my foot entirely off the accelerator and slowed to a stop but kept my foot poised on the clutch, ready to go back into gear. He turned around 180 degrees to get a better look at me with electric blue eyes that cut through the night like a laser as my headlights fell on his face.

Although he was submerged in my lights and his eyes should have been blinded from the proximity of them, he did not cower away from the brightness. He took a few unsteady steps towards me and quickened his pace. I could hear his loud, labouring breaths from inside the car. The air that pushed in and out of his lungs rasped and rattled through his windpipe. But it was the smell that really caught me—it filtered in through the air conditioning. An unmistakeable rotting hum.

Infected. I cursed myself that it had taken this long for the thought to cross my mind.

He was twenty metres away and approaching the bonnet of the car fast when I shoved the gearstick back into first and hammered the accelerator. Within seconds, the car had gathered enough speed that when it made contact with him, his body rebounded off the hood with a sickening crunch. He flew into one of the irrigation ditches at the side of the road. I caught a glimpse of his face before the car made impact and let out an involuntary gasp. His cracked lips were stretched over his teeth in a sneer. His mouth and chin were stained with fresh blood that I had a feeling wasn't his own.

When I arrived home, I made a quick sweep of the car once I had parked it in the garage. There was very little damage to the front; the windscreen and the car's structure were still completely intact with barely a scratch on them. One of the headlights had taken some damage, though. The glass around it was smashed, but the bulb itself was unhurt. I would have to take it to the repair shop tomorrow to have it fixed. If the place was even open.

I entered the house quietly, expecting my family to be asleep, but I was mistaken. Reece was in the living room by herself, her eyes glued to the television. She muted the set as I walked in.

"Everything OK?" she asked. "You don't look too great."

"I've just seen one of them, one of the infected. They're here."

Chapter 19

May 2035

I lay on something hard and unyielding. My spine, pinned beneath the weight of my body, called out to be stretched. I reached out either side of me with aching limbs. My hands met something soft, like tissue. It was toilet paper; it felt shredded. I must be on the floor, I realised. My back was cold. I heard the drip of an open tap nearby.

What happened to me? I wondered, but I couldn't open my eyes. Each time I tried, I was overrun with nausea. My head spun so fast I had to shut them again. I couldn't tell what room I was in, but it must have been the bathroom. The smell of bleach bristled through my nostrils.

"Reece?" I heard Lois's muffled call from somewhere beyond where my feet rested. "Reece, are you in there? Is everything all right?" she called out.

I opened my mouth to reply, the words not coming right away. I felt them croak in the back of my throat. The sound frightened me, reminded me of those months of muted agony when I first woke up. For the slightest moment, panic gripped me as I imagined losing my voice all over again.

"Reece?" she repeated, her voice a little clearer this time. It pulled my thoughts into clarity.

"I'm OK," I murmured, keeping my words as level as possible. "I'm fine, just don't feel too well."

Was it a lie? I didn't think so, but I could hardly call it the truth, either.

Lois took a moment to respond and then finally: "OK, sweetheart. Just let me know if you need anything."

"Thanks," I managed weakly before I had to shut my mouth again, sickness rising up my throat. I listened as she waited a few more seconds, and then her footsteps walked softly away.

⋏

I crept slowly up the stairs, peeking over the bannister at the bathroom door. It was open slightly, but it was dark inside. *Reece must have gone to bed,* I thought. I shot a glance at our bedroom door, firmly closed. No sound came from the other side.

I shuffled into the bathroom, not wanting to wake her if she was resting. The light came on as I crossed the threshold, and I began to get ready for bed too.

As I leant over the sink to wash my face, something caught my eye in the bin below, something red. I rinsed the soap off my skin and patted my cheeks dry. I folded the towel neatly on the warming rail.

I checked the bathroom door was firmly shut and peered into the bin. It was full of tissue, ripped toilet tissue. It looked like somebody had grabbed a toilet roll and bitten through it like an apple. The layers of it shredded completely on one side. I pushed some of it aside, but underneath were more tissues, these dotted with blood.

My heart hammered as I looked around for more damage, but the bathroom was completely intact. Nothing else was broken or looked out of place. I bunched the toilet tissue up and threw it down the pan; the automatic flush carried it away down the waste pipe.

I brushed my teeth, replaced the brush back into its holder, and left the room. The light turned out as I shut the door behind me.

Chapter 20

May 2035
Beijing, China

Using his ophthalmoscope, Doctor Yeung examined the eyes of patient 634. He gave a wordless nod, and the patient was moved on to the next section, pulled along by an armed guard.

Yeung stifled a yawn between patients; another one appeared in front of him, eyes like dinner plates. One small silver lining: it was easier to examine their irises when they were all scared shitless. Apart from when they started crying. The crying ones held up the queue because it took so long for the swelling of their lids to die down. Or the bruised ones. Sometimes they were brought in with big shiners, taking up half their faces. Those ones were almost impossible to scan.

Yeung shoved the patient through the divide and peered to his left for his next one. He didn't meet the eyes of the armed guard as the next person was gripped around the arm and hauled into Yeung's pathway.

A thin green curtain divided each section. Sometimes when the fluorescent lights shone on the curtain from the other side, he could see exactly what was happening in the next "room." It lit up the curtain like a shadow puppet show.

Patient 636 approached, and Doctor Yeung followed the same procedure he had been for the last two days. He checked the pupils for any irregularities and moved the patient along. He yawned again, and his mind wandered to what he might do when he finished his shift later that day.

It was hard to keep focussed when he was drowning in the monotony of a fourteen-hour shift. As he allowed his mind to wander, he wished that he could have been involved in a more exciting element of the process. He longingly thought of the infected camps and the stories he had heard about them. "There is still time," he murmured to himself. If he showed his worth here, then he might get a transfer.

But if he was being honest, he already considered himself worthwhile enough. After all, he was still helping out with the quarantining; that should amount for something regardless of the department he was in. However, he felt like he was above just checking people's eyes.

He liked to ignore the fact that he was one of thousands of doctors who had been ordered to help. He allowed himself to pretend that it was him, solely him, who had been picked out amongst the millions of citizens to be included in the retaliation plan. It made him feel better, and it made him feel important.

At least he was safe down here, he thought to himself. And his stomach balked at the idea of refugees from nearby Mongolia trying to beg their way into China only to be shot down when they refused to turn back. He was relieved that he wasn't involved in that part of the operations. He wasn't sure he was capable of killing somebody.

Patient 637 wore the same green robes that all of the other patients had been issued. She had long black hair tied back from her face. Her bone structure brought Yeung's attention straight to her eyes, and had she not been crying, she might have been quite attractive, Yeung thought.

The robes she wore were too big for her and covered so much of her that the only skin visible was her face and neck. Her head bowed as she was pulled through the curtain. Her body language reeked of submissiveness, just like most of the women who had been brought in.

A young soldier tugged on her arm and hauled her towards Doctor Yeung. She winced but complied with his demand and stood on the yellow X marked on the floor. The soldier stepped back through the curtain to the previous section.

Yeung held up the ophthalmoscope and peered into her eyes, which were still watery with tears. He withdrew the tool and waited for her pupils to clear.

"It's OK," he tried to sooth. But she shook her head, her brow furrowed in fear. She clung to her arm, the one that the soldier had used to pull her forward. "I'll get somebody to look at that for you." Yeung tried to adopt a voice that made him sound tender and caring.

The soldiers could be really rough sometimes, he thought. It had been crossing his mind all day; he wasn't used to such barbarity. But his reasoning was that you *had* to strike some kind of fear into these people or they wouldn't listen. They were more likely to obey your orders if they were scared. And people needed to obey orders if they wanted to get through this process quickly.

Yeung's eyes traced over the angles of her face. He felt for her; he really did. She couldn't have been older than fifteen, still a child. She was pretty. Maybe he could take care of her himself. He tried to make out the shape of her body beneath the gown she wore, but the material fell too loosely over her frame. His spine shivered at the idea of what might be under the green gown, and he coughed to cover up the involuntary groan he felt rising in his throat.

The girl cradled her left forearm; her right hand was wrapped tightly around it. Beneath her hand a dark stain had begun to spread across the material of her robes. She looked guiltily up at Yeung and gave him a limp smile that was full of yellowing, crooked teeth. She had stopped crying.

"Roll back your sleeve," he ordered. The girl shook her head, still grinning. He slapped her across the face and those black eyes of hers widened in mock fear. "Roll back your fucking sleeve."

There was a brief tussle when Yeung grabbed her wrist and began to pull the arm that clutched at the wound beneath her sleeve free. He yanked up the material to reveal a rotting, crescent-shaped wound. The stench was so fierce he felt like he had just taken a punch to the nose. It made him take a step back. It was his turn for his eyes to widen in fear.

He looked from the bite mark to the girl and tried to calculate when those eyes, that had once been so dark, had changed colour.

⸸

I woke up to the sound of several car doors slamming in quick succession. An engine started, and with a screech, the car pulled away. I listened to the roar of the exhaust hurtle out of earshot. I glanced at the clock beside my bed. The dial read 6:12 a.m.

I gently pushed the covers away. A growling headache had gathered at the front of my brain, making me feel like a sledgehammer was being swung against each of my temples simultaneously.

Tenderly, I sat upright and swung my legs around to plant my feet firmly on the floor. The curtains were drawn and most of the room was dark except for a slice of bright light that blasted through a gap between the curtains. It threatened to blind me. I took unsure steps towards the window and looked out onto my neighbourhood below.

Most of the driveways still had cars, and the houses remained seemingly occupied. The house across the road, however, was clearly empty. The windows that had been carefully boarded up last week were now matched with the front door. Two vast boards of wood covered the entryway and its frame, securing the house entirely.

The lack of a car in the driveway and the commotion a few minutes ago indicated that these neighbours had only just left. They were one of the first, though, and it surprised me that after the catastrophe of Michelle March's show that the entire town had not deserted already. I thought it was foolish to leave, though. Wasn't it likely that you would end up going in the wrong direction and heading straight into the storm? You were much safer in an area you knew. At least that was my reasoning.

I scanned the remaining houses that I could see, squinting slightly as those sledgehammers continued to ricochet off my head. I noticed a second family carrying luggage out to their cars. A small boy struggled with a suitcase twice his size until his older sister helped him load it into the boot of their Ford. That family hadn't lived on the street for very long, perhaps only a few months. A father and his two children. I didn't even know their names.

Again I questioned why they would leave a place that they were familiar with. Why leave your own home when it would surely be a better place to store provisions and build fortress-like protection?

Their car was packed. As the two children waited, the father screwed two similarly sized planks of wood across the threshold of their home. When he finished, he shoved the electric drill into the pile of luggage in the back of the car. I imagined the drill being used as a weapon to trepan into the skull of somebody, one of the infected maybe. The thought made my stomach churn.

With a look of trepidation, the neighbour stole a glance towards my home. I'm not sure whether he could see me, but his eyes found my bedroom window and lingered there. His determined expression did not change as he climbed into the car.

They too sped off in the direction of the motorway.

Chapter 21

May 2035

I sprinted upstairs to the bathroom, and my entire body quivered as I ran. I threw open the door, and the light overhead came on automatically, sensing my movement. The door swung open with such force that it rebounded off its hinges and settled back with a gap of a few centimetres from its frame. I didn't have time to close it.

My knees buckled beneath me, and I allowed myself to collapse onto the floor. My body began to twitch and writhe. My back clicked and cracked with the force of my jerking body. Pure agony tore through me, and I bit down hard on my lip to keep from screaming.

The individual cells of my body fought a civil war inside me. One side tried to protect me as the other wreaked havoc in my veins. One side rushed in to repair the damage, and the other shredded my organs like thousands of microscopic bullets rebounding off my arterial walls.

I thought it was the end; it felt like the end. That this was it and I was to die and change right there on that bathroom floor. My thoughts were disjointed. If I spoke them, the words would be incoherent, a brand-new language never spoken before, understood by no one. I felt flooded with a sense of doom, convinced that I would die.

My jaw snapped open and closed, and I bit furiously at the air. I yanked at my own hair, clumps of it coming away in my hands. In my thrashing state, I bit down hard on my own tongue. Blood spilled in my mouth and down the back of my throat.

My eyes flew open. I was ravenous.

I felt a crazed hunger dawn upon me, and I sensed my appetite could only be satisfied by flesh, thick, red, and bloodied flesh. The flesh of the humans I shared a home with. I tried to inhale their scent, closing my eyes with concentration. My nostrils flared as a flowery smell met them. I could feel their presence in the house with me, almost hear their heartbeats, alive, warm. My own heart thudded with excitement at the prospect of peeling the skin from their—

I found myself on my back. Though my eyes were closed, I knew I was on my back, could feel the pressure of the floor against my shoulder blades, knew I was in the bathroom once again. The insatiable hunger I had felt before had abandoned me almost as fast as it had come. I could not remember what it felt like.

I could already feel my joints stiffening under the thick film of my skin and muscle. My body throbbed from the unforgiving states of clenching and unclenching moments before.

When I finally found the strength to sit upright, my head was heavy on my shoulders. Only after some time did I open my eyes again. I shakily stood and checked my reflection in the mirror. My eyes had not changed, not yet anyway, I noticed with some relief.

But my relief was short-lived. Behind me, in the reflection of the mirror, I saw the bathroom door was still open slightly. In the gap stood Jessie, her eyes wide with abject horror, her lips separated into an O shape.

It did not immediately occur to me that Jessie had just seen everything until I watched her begin to back slowly away from the door. Now it was so obvious she had witnessed it all. That flowery smell, it was her perfume.

She had followed me. Of course she had followed me. Of course she was concerned about me. Why wouldn't she be? Wasn't it strange that her mother had run away from her midsentence and disappeared upstairs? Wasn't it strange that her mother had shut herself in the bathroom for prolonged periods, unable to speak as she writhed on the floor in there?

In the several steps Jessie took to reach the stairs, her eyes never left my blood-covered face.

I wondered how differently things would have turned out if I had been able to reach Lois first. Would I have been able to convince Jessie to keep it a secret for much longer than I already had? Would I have changed without their knowing and killed them both in a brutal struggle?

I continued to peer into the mirror above the bathroom sink. I was a mess. My hair was made up of several tangled clumps, and my eyes were bloodshot. I loomed in for a closer look. Since the fits had started, I had been paranoid that my eyes would change colour, but they hadn't yet. That was at least one thing I could cling to. I still had time, even if it was only a little while.

My mouth and tongue were still bleeding. The old blood caked on my chin had begun to dry and crack already, leaving valleys of clean skin between the rivers of blood. I splashed cool water onto my face and allowed my mind to resume some kind of clarity. I gently scrubbed at my chin and cheeks, turning the water in the full basin a rusty brown colour.

When I finished cleaning myself, I shuffled slowly downstairs. My joints and muscles still throbbed from my body's self-assault.

It had been unrealistic to hope that Jessie might not have told Lois everything. As soon as I crossed the threshold, Lois was on me.

"How long?" she demanded, her eyes alight with pure rage.

"A few days…a week…I don't know."

"A week? A fucking week!" Lois exploded. "I knew it. I knew you had been hiding it. A whole fucking week. A whole week and you didn't think to tell us. Did you think it would just go away?"

"No, I—"

"Because shit like this doesn't. You are sick. How long did you think you could ignore it?"

"I was going to tell you both, I promise."

"When? After the next fit? When you're about to turn? When you appear at our bedroom fucking door with that stench and those…those…fucking eyes?" Lois recoiled at the thought of them. It had been by mutual agreement that those blue eyes were the most terrifying part of the virus. Those eyes, so striking in colour, pulsed with hunger and desire, mixed with pure animalistic rage.

I noticed the same rage in Lois's eyes right then.

"Mum, let's call the hotline," Jessie murmured, but Lois flapped her hand in dismissal.

"When were you going to tell us?" She struggled to keep her voice even she was trembling so much.

"I don't know…"

"Well, that is fucking great. Thanks for your consideration."

Her words burnt my face as she hissed them, but I would not look away. I was determined more than ever to hold her gaze. How could she say that? How could she say I didn't consider my family? Consider them was all I had ever done for our entire lives. How could she think that? How could she think that I didn't want what was best for our child?

I had always protected them, had always protected Jessie as much as I could, and I would go on protecting her for as long as I was still alive. I had meant to tell them; I really had. But I had been waiting for the right time. I had been trying to think of a plan. I didn't want to go into quarantine; it was so painfully obvious that it wasn't working, that it would never work until a cure was found. I was going to die. I was going to change into one of those…those things. And the only way it would stop was if I…

"Shoot me," I whispered.

"What?"

"You have to shoot me," I repeated a little louder this time. "You're right. I'm a danger to you both."

Jessie gasped from her position on the sofa, but Lois didn't move. She observed me with the most curious expression on her face, and for a second, I thought she might agree with me. I pushed her further.

"You have that gun from work. You know how to use it too. And I trust you to do it right," I continued, but my voice faltered towards the end.

Lois shook her head. "I won't do it," she finally murmured. She shook her head one final time and looked me directly in the eyes. She repeated her words. "I will not shoot you."

"Please," I begged. "Please at least think about it. We need a solution. I don't want to be one of them. And I don't want to be taken away. I want to be here with you both, but I can't be one of them. Please don't let me get like that. Please."

Unexpected tears sprang from my eyes as I recalled a faint memory of these words being spoken once before. I remembered begging the same thing of Lois when we had seen Alzheimer's patients for the first time after my diagnosis all those years ago. Our doctor had instructed us to go to a home, had told us that it would help to know what was to come. But it had ruined me. I had come home crying, begging for Lois to end my life.

Lois must have remembered this too, because for a second, I witnessed her hardened expression waver.

⁂

And I *could* remember the thought I had had when we had visited the home. And I remembered when Reece was at her worst. Had I not wished that we had made a pact to end Reece's life? Had I not prayed that Reece would die back then? Was this not the same?

But what if my wish had come true back then? Well, Reece would not have taken the cure. We never would have shared this last year together in complete and utter bliss. Then again…if Reece had not taken the cure, then she would have died a long time ago, and we never would have reached this point in our lives at all.

What was more important? Keeping Reece alive in the hope that a cure would soon be found? Or obeying Reece's wish and letting her go now, before the virus took control of her?

⁂

"You will have to do it yourself. I will give you the gun when you are ready. But I won't have any part in murdering my wife," Lois whispered in response. She finally broke eye contact. Her voice was shaking, whether in rage or sadness, I wasn't sure. Neither could I make the same distinction with her tears.

I reached out and took her hand in my own. For the first time, I noticed the greyness of my skin. Lois saw it too, but she did not flinch. I willed her to look into my eyes, but she would not.

"Please, Lois. Please consider it," I repeated once more. I added a final phrase, one that filled me with regret as I spoke because I knew how much it would hurt her. "You owe me."

Chapter 22

May 2035

I swung the car into the first space I found that was close enough to the entrance. Despite the car park's dishevelled appearance, I couldn't bring myself to park outside the white lines provided. It was chaos. There were upturned trolleys, their abandoned food carpeting the surrounding tarmac. Other cars were parked haphazardly and outside the confines of the white lines on the ground; most people hadn't parked at all but had abandoned their cars on the pavement, looking for a quick exit if they needed it. People rushed around like ants; they pushed entire carts full of their shopping. The sight made my stomach drop. We were too late, and everything would be gone.

We had been so engrossed in Reece and so watchful of her that we hadn't left the house in days. Getting supplies hadn't even crossed our minds until this morning. That's why we were out now, praying that at least one shop would be untouched.

We had heard that whole families had uprooted and relocated farther south. Some had even gone through the lengths of leaving the country entirely. They had hijacked boats and illegally crossed the English Channel. We had watched it on television as it unfolded. Only a few dedicated news reporters remained, and they captured the country's descent into chaos.

Reece and I had decided to stay put and fortify our home despite whatever danger she might pose to us. We had found some old planks of wood in the garage and had reinforced the windowpanes and door frames downstairs. Jessie and I had sneaked out late one night to steal rings of barbed wire off the fences surrounding the local industrial estates. We reattached the wire so it ran across the top of our own fence that skirted the back garden.

Moving somewhere else would only cause more disruption, and that might mean less time with Reece as a human being. Nobody was even sure that other parts of the country were safer than where they were currently residing. There were rumours about safer parts of Europe, but they hadn't been proven to be true. And it didn't make sense. We were an island. Surely it would be safer here than on the mainland?

As for the town we lived in, those who had packed their bags and driven off in various directions of the country had no real proof that where they were going was any better than where they had been. They drove in blind faith but were sure to encounter long tailbacks of traffic as everybody else followed suit. And then what? As they waited in their cars for the traffic to clear, they would be sitting ducks, easy targets.

Since that night after work when I had driven home, I hadn't encountered any of the infected. It seemed as if we were safe for a little while yet. Or we had just been incredibly lucky.

And since our conversation, I had been unwilling to talk about the imminent possibility of Reece's change. I could not bear Reece's suggestion, and I rebuffed all of her attempts to discuss it as well as her prompts to reveal the location of my gun. I had agreed to let her do it to herself, but I wasn't ready yet. Her words had hurt me; she had used my own guilt against me in a bid to change my mind.

No matter how many times Reece warned me that she would change soon, I had not even dignified her with a response. I couldn't. I was terrified. I didn't want to give her the gun and then face the possibility of finding her body, still warm, a hole in the roof of her mouth, particles of her brain sprayed on the ceiling.

The thought of it made me physically sick, but I had to come around to it. I had to. We were running out of time.

It was unlike me to hide my head in the sand, and I knew that. I had become familiar with my own decisiveness. I flourished on the feeling of productivity. But this wasn't the same. I still wanted to believe that a cure could be found before Reece changed. The longer I thought about it, the more

I thought that I wasn't able to go through with it. I couldn't kill her. Just like before, it went against all of my instincts. But she was right. I *did* owe her. I owed her the end she so desperately craved.

"Are you ready?" Jessie asked. A few minutes had passed since I had parked the car, and I hadn't moved yet. Out of the corner of my eye, I could see her knees knocking together they were trembling so hard. I nodded and checked the clasp on my holster. It was secure and tight across my body. I wore a jacket made from light material over the top of it so it was concealed, but I would still be able to access the weapon easily.

"Yeah, I think so." My reply was slow, a little unsure. I ran my finger over the handle of my gun to check that there was definitely a magazine in it. I wasn't even sure why I had brought the thing, but to leave the gun behind entirely and leave us at risk without any method of defence should the worst happen, well, that was foolish.

And there was the thought of what Reece might have done unsupervised with it should she have found it. My whole body shuddered.

My stomach clenched at the idea of her home alone. In the one day since she suggested her idea, she had already deteriorated significantly. Her skin was a washed-out grey colour, and her cheeks were hollow. Her frizzy hair thinned at the temples, and what was left was greasy, slick with dirt. She hadn't showered.

As we left, she promised to lock and deadbolt the internal door between the kitchen and the garage behind us. And only once I had heard the bolt slide home and the key in the lock had I opened the electric garage door.

When Reece had been stronger, she had cleared enough space in the garage so that our car could be parked inside. It was Jessie who had first suggested parking it there; she had picked it up from the various news stories that had been running twenty-four-hours a day. The garage had become an airlock; we could drive in, shut the electric door remotely from the car, and once we were sure it was safe to get out, we could, straight into the safety of our garage. Then we would enter the house via the personnel door and lock it behind us.

It was safe and effective. At least we hoped it was. It had been too early to tell, but the prospect of trialling it was looming closer as the infection's toll grew in size day by day.

"Remember our plan?" I asked.

Jessie nodded in reply.

"And what should you do if I don't get back to the designated place within the designated time?"

"Return to the car, load up, and wait for three more minutes."

"And what do you have to do in the car?" I prompted.

"Find a weapon and lock the doors."

"Well done. And if the three minutes are up and I'm not at the car in time?"

Jessie paused, and I heard a gulp come from her throat. "Jessie?"

"I leave," she said, and her voice trembled.

"Good. Well then, let's go."

Jessie and I hopped out of the car in unintentional sync. We carefully observed the area around us; we appeared to be surrounded by only healthy people. Healthy people, but stressed people. I made a cursory glance at each person to see if they might be cradling cuts on their bodies. Nobody seemed to be.

We paused to listen out for any noises that might resemble the moans of the sick. We were safe in that respect too. Only the panicked murmur of human voices surrounded us.

Our aim was simple: to get in, grab as much food as we could carry, and get out unscathed. Whether there would be food still in there was a different matter. We had considered the possibility of allowing Reece to drive—she could wait for us in the car as a getaway driver. But it was eventually decided that she was far too sick. Unable to stand for longer than a few minutes, she would have been useless driving.

I gave Jessie a nod and stroked the gun in its holster one last time. We advanced towards the hypermarket. On entering, we found it just as chaotic as the car park. Abandoned trolleys littered the aisles and damaged products had been further crushed and dented underfoot as they had fallen off the half-desecrated shelves. I was relieved to find that the food shelves were not quite as bare as we expected. In their greed, looters had gone straight for expensive items; laptops, TVs, and smartphones were all missing from their displays.

I praised these shortsighted people who believed that they would still have the luxury of electricity in a few weeks' time. It meant the useful things, the cans of food and pasta, were mostly still intact.

As agreed, Jessie raced off to the farthest end of the store while I darted along the first few aisles. When our predetermined fifteen minutes were up, we reconvened by the tills. Our trolleys were piled high with duct tape, string, and various cans of food, bottled water, and several different-sized kitchen knives. Jessie gave me a sly grin as she approached.

"I went out the back to the stockroom. There were tonnes of stuff, all untouched. A delivery must have just come in, but nobody had put it out," she told me, her voice smug. "Let's go, Mum."

"I just want to…" I began. I looked over at the checkouts and patted my pockets.

"Come on, Mum. Nobody else is paying," Jessie said. She raised her eyebrows and nodded towards the hordes of people who hadn't been so forthcoming in paying for their goods. Those who had baskets full of products were running straight for the store exit and were not being stopped; there was nobody to stop them.

I wanted to leave that shop without further thought, just like everyone else. But I just couldn't bring myself to do it. I was not a person who stole by nature. I was a police officer, for goodness sake. It felt alien to me, breaking the law. As we approached the exit, I imagined walking into work in a month's time, when this had all blown over, and being hauled into my boss's office to receive a written warning. Him showing me CCTV footage of us leaving the shop without paying.

I stopped.

"Mum? Come on."

"Just…just wait for one second," I replied. I parked my trolley next to hers and went back to the bank of checkouts and took out four fifty-pound notes and stuffed them under one of the tills. The black cloud of guilt that I had carried to the exit dispersed. Despite the fact I knew the money would be stolen should it be found there, it comforted me to know that I had at least tried to pay. And if I was reprimanded by anyone, then I could show the camera footage, and it would all be OK.

My conscience clear, we left the store too. Jessie let out a breath of impatience when I returned to her, but I ignored it. We pushed and dragged our shopping with us at a leisurely pace; there didn't seem to be any danger, and our car was in sight.

We were one row away from it when we heard the first screams.

At the sound, Jessie faltered and took her hands off the trolley, but I quickened my pace, grabbing the front of hers and hauling it along with me. As we ran, I observed the people around me as closely as I could. At the first scream, the crowds began to move fast, and like us, they threw themselves in the direction of their vehicles. Those who lacked the nerve and were close enough jumped into their cars immediately and abandoned their goods. Others who knew they had more time unloaded their belongings as fast as they could.

Two metres from the car, I prodded the button on my keys and the boot flew open. I hurled myself towards it, throwing things into the boot faster than I thought possible. Jessie helped.

I looked back at the store. Those who were leaving had begun to sprint away from it; they carried heavy loads of shopping in their reusable canvas bags. Others who had only just arrived at the store weighed their options. They could go home empty-handed and survive on whatever they had in their homes already. Or they could make an attempt to take whatever they could find in the shop now and face the consequences when they dared to return to their cars. Many opted for the first option; they hoped that other nearby shops would still be safe.

I couldn't tell where the screams were coming from, made worse by the fact that they were becoming more frequent and the panic around us was increasing further. Originally, I could have judged that the attacks were coming from our left, but now it felt like the cries were striking us from all directions. My throws became more and more frantic the louder the screams became.

My ears pricked as the moans that were once too far away to be heard were now closing in. I ordered Jessie to keep an eye around us, but I couldn't help but look myself.

My eyes were drawn to the next row of cars where a woman was already pinned to the floor, shrieking for help, a car door open next to her. A man had clamped his jaws firmly around her wrist and attempted to separate a chunk of flesh from her arm. A young girl no older than nine who must have been her daughter watched desperately from the back seat of their car. She went unnoticed by the animals around her, who were closing in on the woman, attempting to feed on her from all angles. The girl howled desperately, her blond pigtails swinging frantically as she bobbed her head around, trying to get a closer look.

My movements slowed, and I prayed that the girl would be quiet, would stop drawing attention to herself. I felt sick, and I wanted to look away or help or just do something, anything, but I was frozen. For a moment, her blond pigtails turned to bunches of brown curly hair. Her skin had darkened, a loop of baby fat around her middle…my heart plummeted. I shook my head, dissolving the image. The girl switched back to her white-skinned self, and the blond hair returned.

It is one thing to watch the attacks on television, I thought to myself. At least when it was on there, you could pretend you were just watching some hyped-up Hollywood movie, but to see it in person was entirely different. The smell alone was stifling; the stench of rotting flesh invaded my nose and the back of my throat. The chorus of groans had become ear-splittingly loud. The hairs on the back of my neck stood up at the sound of their rasping breaths floating over the tops of the cars.

"Fuck, fuck, fuck," I hissed under my breath. "Let's go, now." I launched the remaining items in my trolley onto the back seat of the car, and I shoved the cart roughly away. It clattered with an unforgiving crunch into a nearby parked car.

Metres away, one of the attackers who had been feasting on the woman's torn-open stomach stopped his assault abruptly. His head snapped up and cocked to one side. There was an intelligence in his face that I had not anticipated.

Between his lips was a chunk of half-eaten intestine. The rest of it dribbled out of his mouth. And his eyes, they were that shocking pale blue. The exact same colour as the man I had hit with my car, but the irises seemed brighter this time, now that we were closer.

At the sight of Jessie and me and the prospect of even fresher and still-conscious meat, he leapt to his feet and began to half run, half stagger towards us. His body was shaking so hard with desire at our untouched flesh it made my own shiver.

"*Fucking run!*" I screamed. I sprinted to my side of the car as Jessie ran to hers. I threw open the door and leapt in. I jabbed the button on the dashboard to start the car and looked over at Jessie's side to check she was strapped in.

My heart stopped; the seat was empty.

Jessie screamed and bashed her closed fists against the car window, and I jumped. Her door had failed to open. It was still locked. I stabbed at the central locking button on my key fob, but the lock still wouldn't budge.

She was already crying, her eyes begging me for help. I slammed my own door shut and leaned over to fumble with the lock. I tried to pull the knob up. The creature…animal…

whatever the fuck it was, was barely a metre away from Jessie when the door finally released, and she threw herself in. But before she could slam it shut, the man had launched himself towards her. His teeth chattered and threatened to clamp down on the closest part of her body.

"Help me!" she screamed. Tears poured down her face as she tried to kick out at the monster and make him lose his grip. She landed one firm punch into his neck; it made him stutter backwards, but it was not enough.

I plunged my hand into my jacket and pulled at the gun. I half expected it to jam itself within the strap of its holster, but it came free easily. It was heavy in my hand. I hadn't had a chance to use it in action yet, had only ever done so in training. What if I missed?

This man's movements were sharp, and his head jerked from side to side, trying to get a purchase on Jessie's flesh. He was so close that I could see his bloodstained teeth and the cracks of blood in the creases of his face. His smell was so rancid that I felt myself dry-heaving. I fleetingly wondered how long he had been dead.

His companions who had noticed the commotion were closing in on the car too, their piercing eyes locked on to Jessie's flailing body. Her bare hip had worked itself loose from under her T-shirt, and I watched the guy's tongue flip across his lips in anticipation. The thought made bile rise into my mouth.

I looked across the car park and saw the car from earlier, the driver's door still wide open. The dashboard lit up with warning lights. The cracked windscreen was smeared with blood, the back seat empty. I looked around desperately for the little girl, and just as I had begun to convince myself that she had miraculously escaped and allowed myself to look away, I caught the eye of a small figure. She was four feet tall with long blond pigtails. Her mouth was open in a high-pitched moan. Her lips and denim dungarees were already stained with blood. A gigantic bite wound spanned her entire tiny forearm. I looked into her unblinking stare and shivered.

The image of Jessie returned in her place. Jessie in her uniform, getting ready for her first day at school. The pleated skirt and white shirt pristine except for the stains of blood on them. Her face the same, just as it had been at five years old, but her eyes weren't brown, and in her mouth were a set of blood-drenched baby teeth. The thought brought me out of my reverie.

"Fucking shoot it!" Jessie hollered, but I continued to freeze. The entire scene felt painfully slow. Jessie's legs kicked and lashed out at the man as if she were under water. Her attempts to pull the door shut moved so slowly that it was almost comical when the door rebounded off his thick frame. His teeth were mere inches from her bare ankle, sluggishly chomping at the air as he got closer to her. And that bare section of her hip…a nine-year-old Jessie, in dungarees, her dark hair in two bunches either side of her head, flashed before my eyes, and I squeezed the trigger.

The gun fired, and Jessie screamed and snatched her hands away from the door handle as if she had been burnt.

The one and only shot had taken a lump off the man's head, and he collapsed back onto the pavement. I leaned over her and slammed the door, ramming the lock back down.

"Are you bitten?" I demanded, my senses demisted.

"I don't know...I don't..." she sobbed, not even looking down at her legs. Her eyes were drawn to her hands and the bloodstains from where she had punched a piece of flesh free from the man's cheek.

"Are you fucking bitten?" I repeated. Shouting over the volume of dozens of hands pounding on the metal frame and windows of the car.

"No, no! I'm not. I don't—" Jessie began, but I had stopped listening. I shoved the gearstick into first and took one last look around to absorb the scene. Those who had taken the risk of going inside for more supplies would not come out lucky. When they tried to return to their cars, they would find the car park swarming with the infected. Some people had already tried to battle their way out of the supermarket but had not been successful, their stolen loot weighing them down.

The lucky ones were taken early—they didn't have to be spectators to their friends and family or even themselves being eaten alive. The lucky ones had their heads cracked on the pavements, resulting in such quick and ruthless deaths that they did not have to experience the feeling of their brains being scooped out of their skulls like a fruit salad at a buffet.

I thrust my foot onto the accelerator and eased my foot off the clutch, desperate not to stall the engine and waste more time. The gunshot had piqued the interest of more infected nearby. They began to shuffle towards the car, crooked fingers outstretched. Just as they started to hammer on the windows, I rammed my foot harder on the pedal, full throttle, and the car lurched forward. Its tyres screamed, slicing a valley through the horde. The car moved with such a sudden force that it left a stinking cloud of rubbery smoke in the air behind us.

Near the exit of the car park, I could see two uninfected people shouting and jumping up and down. They called out to us, and as we rocketed over the speed bump, their desolate faces loomed in towards the car. They leaned in and thundered on the bodywork trying to get our attention, snatching at the door handles. They begged to be picked up, but I drove furiously on, speeding in the direction of home.

I didn't let off the pedal until our house was in sight. After the frenzy at the supermarket, the streets on our way home seemed eerily quiet in comparison. The roads were bare, save for a few cars hurtling in the opposite direction. Jessie cried softly the entire journey home, her face bright red and puffy by the time we parked in the garage.

We had come so close to death Jessie had even felt the foul ragged breath of it on her skin. I could not bear to think about what might have happened if I hadn't had my gun or hadn't reached it in time. I cursed my delayed reactions in shooting that animal, but it could have been worse. If I had been unable to pull the gun from its sleeve, then a different scenario entirely would have played out.

My heart broke at the possibility of Jessie being hurt or killed because I had not been able to stop it. She was scared now, mentally, and I knew that was my fault. I hadn't moved fast enough. Now neither of us would ever be able to get those images out of our minds.

My thoughts drifted to Reece—one day soon she would pose the same danger to us. It was only a matter of time before she changed from human to…whatever they were. And what would we do if we didn't realise in time? The transition of Alzheimer's patients into AZ-infected beasts had been unpredictable, hadn't it? That's why it had become so deadly and spread so quickly initially. Nobody had seen it coming. And those who had seen it hadn't bothered to react.

One week, everybody who had taken the drug was happy and healthy and had overcome a life-threatening illness… and then the next, they were mindless cannibals. Whereas those who developed the infection from a bite—their changes were almost immediate. You could count the number of seconds before they transformed. That was proved by what I had seen with that little girl earlier.

Our only saving grace was that we could see Reece's deterioration, could see her hair thinning, her skin greying. But how much farther must she go down that road before she reached the end? She could be in bed with me or we could be watching television as a family, and then suddenly she might leap on us and tear our flesh from our bones. Jessie would suffer the same fate as that little girl. My stomach dropped. I just couldn't get that kid out of my head.

Despite Jessie's advancing age, in my thoughts she would always be a little four-year-old girl in her first ever two-sizes-too-big uniform. My mind flicked from one distant memory to another, like an old reel of film. In the next slide, I saw her hiding behind Reece at Disneyland because the dressed-up characters had scared her. The one after I saw her howling with distress on the doorstep of my parents' house, reluctant to be left for a weekend, Reece hugging her and rubbing her back to sooth her cries.

Jessie wasn't strong-willed as I was; she was gentle and kind like Reece, but she was fragile too. She needed assurance and care. And when she had been growing up, it had been Reece who had supplied that, an endless flow of encouragement and cuddles. I had stood back and felt alienated and excluded; these feelings of distress and anxiety that they bonded over felt foreign to me. It was a level of relationship that I couldn't reach. I could not mollycoddle Jessie in the way that Reece had. I showed my caring side in other ways. I paid the bills. I made the dinner…subtle things. Important things.

I imagined the little girl's mother and how she had been so close to getting in the car too. I imagined the woman's dying thoughts as she hoped that her daughter might go unnoticed and be safe. Perhaps the mother had even thought she could fight a few of them off and kill them. Isn't that what all parents strived for with their children? To fight their battles, to keep them safe from harm. To protect them. It didn't matter what age they were, parents felt like they had a responsibility to keep their children away from danger, big or small.

Keeping Reece alive would mean keeping Jessie in danger. It kept both of us in danger. What kind of mother would I be if I ignored the problem that we faced? I couldn't just let Reece change suddenly and then attack us at will, knowing that I could have prevented it all. No, I had a responsibility to look after our daughter in the way that Reece had always looked after her, in the way that that mother looked after her child in the car park.

There was not much more I could do for Reece; there was no hope left for her. But for my daughter and for myself, there was still plenty to live for and still plenty to do to make sure we survived unscathed.

I would do anything for my daughter.

I put the car into neutral and switched the engine off. The electric door rattled shut behind us. I gave the horn a light push to announce our arrival to Reece. The blasting noise pulled Jessie from her sobs, and she began to compose herself, ready to get out of the car.

Minutes passed and panic began to rise in my throat. We were too late. Something must have happened to Reece. She must have changed while we were gone. My palms began to sweat at what might be waiting for us on the other side of that door. We would have to go in through the front; this way was locked from the inside.

I sensed Jessie's eyes on me, watching me closely.

"You wait here. I'll check on her," I muttered, my heart in my mouth. I retrieved the gun from its holster where I had replaced it after the initial shooting. I checked the magazine again just to be sure. I couldn't remember how many bullets it had taken to execute Jessie's attacker before, but a quick count told me I had only used one.

I opened the car door slowly and tried to listen for any noises inside the house. The air was still. I crept over to the internal door and pressed my ear against it. I cursed my actions earlier when I had beeped the horn. The noise seemed unbelievably loud now that I thought about it. Anybody could have heard it, any of those things out there.

Faintly, I could hear the muffled shuffling of a pair of feet approaching the door. Had Reece's footsteps already been reduced to shuffles before we left the house? Had she been walking the determined footsteps of the healthy before? I took a step back and raised my gun towards it. I aimed it where I knew Reece's head would be. Decades of our lives together reassured me that my estimation of her height would be true.

The footsteps on the other side of the door came to a stop. Slowly, the bolts and locks on the other side of the door began to shake and rattle as they were opened. I could barely hear them over the noise of my heart banging in my ears. Could the dead open doors? I questioned myself and thought of the girl with pigtails. But I remembered that she had been in the car with the door already open.

There had been rumours that there were smarter versions of the dumbstruck infected that were roaming the streets. There were further rumours that the true cause of the outbreak was that the AZ drug overstimulated the minds of those who took it and sent their brains into destructive overdrive. The takers became too smart, their memories too good. Their intellectual talents increased at such a phenomenal rate that their neurons could no longer take it. Their brains fried inside their skulls as they became victims of this new plague.

The locks stopped rattling, and there was a pause. I thought of that scene in *Jurassic Park* when the characters realise that the velociraptor is smart enough to open doors and recalled their panicked eyes as they looked down at the door handle to see it moving. I held my breath and waited.

My gun hand shook with nerves. The door opened slowly, and I was met with Reece's hallowed face. The grey hue of her skin made her natural colour undetectable. She opened her mouth to speak but only emitted a croaking sound in place of words.

I forced myself to make eye contact. Those beautiful hazel eyes that I had fallen in love with all those years ago, would they still be there? Those beautiful hazel eyes that swam with tears so often when Reece was sick but were normally strong and resilient before the Alzheimer's, were they still present in that aged face?

I could hardly stand the thought of her eyes being that horrific blue instead. We locked gazes, and I let out a grateful sigh. They were unchanged. Reece was unchanged. And I was so thankful that I threw myself at Reece and embraced her before I had even checked for any of the other ghoulish symptoms.

"I'll do it," I announced as soon as the three of us sat together in the living room. Reece and I on one sofa and Jessie on the other. The TV played in the background, the sound on mute. Frightening images flashed on the screen, and I wondered how the stations had got hold of the footage. It seemed to be amateur, like somebody's home movies.

"What?" Reece's drawn and tired face flickered with confusion.

"I won't let you kill our daughter. I've just seen those... those *things* up close, and I...I just can't stand the thought of you being like that. They tried to get her," I whispered. I cast a sidelong look at Jessie; her head was bowed, her body quivering like a frightened rabbit. "They were so close she would have died if I hadn't had my gun with me and if we hadn't been prepared. We might not be so lucky if you...*when* you change."

"I know," Reece groaned. The noise bordered on unhuman, and for half a minute afterwards, we regarded each other wordlessly. The groan had had such an animalistic tone to it that it reminded me so vividly of what I had just witnessed in the car park; I shivered. Reece made a movement to reassure me but stopped. She nodded and shuffled away from me.

Jessie's sobs had reached a fever pitch. I could tell that she was replaying the trauma of what had just happened to her, and I knew it would stay with her for months, if not years. It would only get worse after what would happen in the following hours.

"When?" I whispered. The question was almost unintelligible beneath the sound of our daughter.

"I think it will be soon, but I can't tell. It's only what I've read online. And nobody is posting anything new on there anymore. It's like the Internet has gone down entirely," Reece replied.

Almost as if the house had heard her, the TV cut out and the lights above us switched off. Jessie looked up from her hands momentarily to absorb the sight of the now-blank screen. She dipped back down again and sobbed harder than before.

"A few days maybe," Reece added. Her eyes searched my face.

Chapter 23

May 2035

Hours had passed since we had arrived home from our ordeal at the store. Reece and I agreed that we would discuss our plan of action tomorrow after we had all had some rest. We lit candles and placed them sporadically around the ground floor of the house. We ate dinner together, and Reece collapsed on the sofa, exhausted. Jessie sat on the opposite sofa, both of them completely drained by the day's events.

I stayed in the kitchen, never too far away from my daughter, and unpacked the food we had taken. As I filled the cupboards, I tried to come to terms with what might happen in the next few days. I pictured Reece on her knees, my gun in my hand ready to execute her. The thought filled me with dread, but I knew I would have to face it soon. I couldn't keep hiding from it; we had made an agreement now, and I wouldn't go back on it.

After I unpacked, I took a seat at the kitchen table and rested my head in my hands. I pictured our entire lives together. How we met, how we got married, how we tried for a baby and eventually had Jessie. I remembered the desolation we had both felt when Reece was diagnosed with Alzheimer's and the elation Jessie and I had shared when the cure had been announced.

I remembered Reece and I buying this house together, our first house. And I remembered our wedding day. The thoughts choked the back of my throat, and I had to force my eyes shut to keep the tears from pouring down my face.

I thought back to the days when Reece's disease was at its worst, and I remembered how I had prayed for her to die. I remembered how I had considered the possibility of killing her. How I wish I hadn't thought of it so lightly back then, now that the possibility had become a reality.

I fell asleep reminiscing on the happier times of our life, going back to our wedding day again and the birth of our daughter. I regretted all the time I had wasted at work when I should have been with my wife and my young daughter. I pictured Reece in her beautiful white gown, the sun making her brown skin glow, and the slight pinkness in her cheeks as she walked up the aisle towards me. She had been more terrified than I that day. The same anxious signs appearing on her that Jessie showed now. Teary eyes, pounding heart.

I thought of baby Jessie, so small and so perfect. And how we couldn't stop staring at her from the moment she had arrived. We would huddle over her crib and coo over her long eyelashes and those tiny curls on top of her head.

I rested my own head on the table and slowly drifted into an unconscious oblivion.

Hours later I opened my eyes. Something had roused me from sleep, but I was too groggy to remember what it was.

I waited, and there it was again. The sound turned the blood in my veins to ice. As I thought of her name, she called for me.

"Mum!" I heard her scream. That one word was enough to send me rocketing from my chair, instinctively pressing my hand against the cool metal of the gun I still had strapped around my body. I released the holster's catch and rested my palm on the handle.

There was no training on earth that could have prepared me for what I found in the next room. That all-too-familiar rotting smell had already started emitting itself from Reece's prone body. I had missed the convulsions altogether. Reece lay still, her eyes closed. Next to her, a candle lay on the floor, its wax half crushed and the wick flameless.

Jessie still screamed; she bent down next to Reece. By the looks of the mess of blankets on the sofa, they had both been asleep, but Reece had managed to spasm her way into the middle of the room. Jessie stretched her arms out to Reece, wanting to wake her, wanting to check she was OK. It was a knee-jerk reaction, and I have never blamed her for it.

"Don't move. Don't touch her," I warned.

If I had had any sense, then I would have drawn my gun fully almost as soon as I heard that first scream. I guess if I had been thinking straight, I would have shot Reece before her eyes even reopened and before she began those haunting, rattled breaths. But I had been out of my mind all afternoon since the incident at the supermarket, and I had had the blind faith that the virus might not claim Reece until we had made our plans. How stupid I was.

What I'm describing all happened in the space of thirty seconds, but it felt like hours. I imagined that family in Georgia, the one whose grandmother murdered and ate her own granddaughter. I imagined how the child wouldn't have had a chance in her proximity to the animal. Jessie would not have a chance where she stood right now.

Before I could call out to her and tell her to move, before Jessie even realised what was happening, Reece snatched at Jessie's arm with her gnarled and greyed hand. It was the closest part of Jessie that could be reached. And in her crouched pose, just one tug was all that was needed to send her spiralling to the ground. Reece was on her in seconds.

Before she leapt upon our daughter, she flashed me a look with those eyes, almost like she knew what she was. Like she knew what she was about to do and wasn't completely mindless.

Those eyes. The green flecks that were once so breathtaking to me were now steel grey. The deep brown, amongst the green flecks that I would often lose myself in, had transformed into that terrifying electric blue. It was exactly the colour I had seen in the eyes of all the others.

In the eyes of the man I ran over and the man I shot as he tried to murder my daughter, in the eyes of the little girl in the car park. And yet, seeing the colour this close was different; it made my heart stop. It really was just as striking as they had all said. In the time between the incident at the hypermarket and now, I had forgotten how enchanting and entirely chilling those eyes were.

My mind flashed back to *The March Show* and that humid day last week when Michelle March was eaten alive by a horde of them. My stomach rolled.

I don't know why Reece went for Jessie first. Maybe it was because she was closer than I. Maybe it was Jessie's harrowing screams that tempted her and wound her up to a fever pitch of desire. I will never find out. She knew both of us were in that room at that moment. And I knew that because of the way she looked at me with those bright blue eyes.

It was a look of knowing. It was a look of retribution. It was a look that said, "You stopped loving me. You wanted me dead all those years ago, and now this is my revenge."

It was a look that shook me right to the very depths of my soul.

Jessie began to roll with Reece across the carpet in a bid to fight her off. Jessie was strong, but she was uncoordinated, and she lacked the fierce determination of a starved and crazed human. As they flailed across the floor, Reece's body slammed into the coffee table. A sickening smack, Jessie's right fist connected to Reece's face, and it made me snap out of my trance. Reece's bloodied spit sprayed across the room. I felt the warmth of it on my face.

"Shoot her!" Jessie screamed at me.

Her punch had not deterred Reece in the slightest; she was still snapping at my daughter. Only held off by Jessie's raised knees, keeping Reece's mouth just inches from the flesh of her neck. Had Reece been at her old strength, way back when she hadn't even been diagnosed with Alzheimer's, Jessie would not have stood a chance.

"Shoot her!" Jessie roared again. I admired her determination now, how her fear for her life was so strong that she wasn't thinking twice about the death of her mother. How she wasn't thinking that it would be me who had to fire the gun and how it might fuck me up entirely.

In her eyes, the death must have already happened. She wasn't seeing Reece right now; she had detached herself from that, I realised.

I took aim, but they were moving around too much. Each time I thought I had a good lock on Reece's head, Jessie's body moved into my line of vision, blocking the shot. To make the situation worse, my arm was shaking furiously.

I had just two thoughts before I fired. Jessie, four years old in her school uniform. And Reece on our wedding day, the white of her dress that made her dark skin glow. I knew I had to lose one of them, and I knew which one it had to be. I just couldn't lose both.

I fired two shots, maybe three. It could have been four. But after those shots, the tussle stopped immediately. My wife and my daughter, my family. They both lay sprawled side by side.

My heart roared in my ears, but my breathing had stopped. The gun was still raised, and my arms shook with the force of an earthquake.

On the floor, one of them had taken a headshot. Blood spilled out around her body. The other lay completely still except for the laboured heaving of her chest.

Chapter 24

An unspecified date, several months after the first reported outbreak

My eyes opened suddenly, my heart drumming. I did not know whether it was day or night because of the large wooden planks nailed across the windows of the house. The gap between them was not enough to let the light in, and the darkness terrified me, but I had no other choice if I wanted to remain safe. With shaking hands, I lit the candle next to me, relieved to find myself alone.

I thought of the plankless windows in the bedroom above. I had used them to spy on whatever was outside many times before.

I had seen the infected push their hands through the smallest gaps to reach at whatever live flesh they could find. I had seen the healthy dragged from their cars and my neighbours torn to pieces in front of my very eyes. Those who had declined to evacuate because they couldn't bear to leave their homes behind…they had been the first to go. They had neglected to put the proper defences in place, and those things out there…they had broken the windows and poured in through the empty frames. They had eaten any living thing that screamed loud enough for them to find. Like a sick game of Marco Polo.

My neighbours had had their intestines ripped from their stomachs and swallowed greedily by those…those monsters. Did they have names? I wasn't sure. I hadn't heard another person speak in weeks. I was unsure if I could even talk anymore. My words had died in my throat, and I wondered if I might ever have the chance to say them again.

There was a faint scream outside…no…not a scream. It was more like a howl, I decided. Like a wounded dog, crying for its owner. I couldn't bear that noise; it penetrated my thoughts in the daytime and breached the sanctity of my dreams at night. The nightmares I had were terrifying enough on their own, but when I woke to the sounds of those creatures outside, I realised the nightmares were nothing compared to reality. At least in my dreams, I wasn't alone. My brain produced people, companions to protect me, to listen to me, to make me laugh. And when I woke up, they vanished.

Now I could barely think because the howling was so loud. I had to drown the noise out. I must find something to do to push their cries from my ears. It was beginning to make me feel sick; my head was beginning to spin.

I crept upstairs and flicked on the portable radio and was met with an eerie silence. I tried to remind myself that I had expected the quiet, in a bid to make myself feel less isolated. But it still didn't stop the crippling sting of loneliness and the prickling sensation of tears. With a deep breath, I fiddled with the tuner dial on the set and listened carefully.

I was met with more silence, some white noise, and silence again and again…and then finally, just when I thought I would give up and turn the radio off altogether, I heard what I had been searching for. A human voice.

"…doors and windows. Help is coming…

"Attention, attention please. This is an emergency broadcast for the United Kingdom. This is not a test. There has been a nationwide emergency situation, which has triggered this message. The present conditions of the country are dangerous and hazardous to human health.

"There is an unknown virus that has infected much of the country's population. This virus is highly dangerous and can be transmitted through a bite from infectious persons. Citizens of the United Kingdom are advised to stay inside and lock their doors and windows. Do not attempt to approach infected persons.

"This is not a test. Citizens are advised to stay inside and lock their doors and windows. Help is coming…

"Attention, attention please. This is an—"

And so it continued endlessly, alternating between male and female voices. Both professional, both robotic in their speech. Each time the radio began another repetition, I hoped that it would say something different. I hoped that a real human would interrupt and speak instead of these stupid metallic voices.

Help was coming. How long had they been promising that? When did this announcement start going out? How do they know who is still out there? I imagined the possibility of being found. Dozens of camo-clad soldiers would burst into the house. "It's all right, madam. You're safe now. Help is here." I laughed low and desperately at my own hopeful imagination.

I reached over to the radio and turned it off. "Help is coming." I repeated it over and over to myself. "Help will be here soon. I will be safe." Tears began to roll down my cheeks, gently at first and then faster and faster until they would not stop. I began to howl; I howled just like those monsters outside. I knew better than to make a sound. I had been so careful to be quiet and to remain invisible, but my sobs were uncontrollable. They were unrelenting no matter how many deep breaths I took.

In my desperation, I almost hoped that they would hear me and that they would find me so I could be put out of my misery. Would it really be so bad to become one of them? It would be quick. I knew that much. I had seen them change before my very eyes, so I knew it was a matter of seconds.

Sure, they rolled around a bit; they might even be in pain. But once they'd changed, the pain must be forgotten. At least that's what it seemed like. I never saw any of them crying about their dislocated jaws or their rotting limbs. They only knew one thing, and that was the desire for the flesh of the living.

Finally, after what seemed like hours, I stopped crying abruptly. I wiped my eyes; they were sore from my moment of hysteria. I tried to gain some clarity. Something had made me stop crying, but what had it been?

After a moment's hesitation, I regained control of my breathing just like I had been told to do. The breathing helped; it always calmed me down. And in the silence, I realised that it was a noise that had made me stop crying. It was a very small, slight sound. It was almost insignificant and unremarkable. But I had been alive through this long enough to know that this noise was unmistakeable, and it could not be ignored.

They were coming.

Acknowledgements

First and foremost, I would like to thank every single person who helped in the writing, editing, and designing process. Your hard work and professionalism is greatly appreciated.

I would like to thank my parents for believing in this dream and for being just as excited as I am about it. I would like to thank my brothers, who kept me grounded throughout the writing of *Side Effects May Vary*, and Timmy, who always gave me an excuse to take a break. I would like to thank Nick, Nicole, and SJ, who have always been tremendously supportive of all of my endeavours, no matter how silly.

Most importantly, I would like to acknowledge my grandma for her bravery in the face of Alzheimer's and my grandad for his courage. It has been a childhood dream to write a book, and my heart breaks that I cannot share it with you.

Lastly, I want to thank Chloe. Although you haven't finished this journey with me, you started it by listening patiently to my ideas (good or bad), supporting me, and being an unwitting source of encouragement when I wanted to give up. I never would have made it this far without you.

About the Author

Born in 1992 in Southampton, Ellis Reid now lives in Brighton and owns sixty-two cats. They are all named after characters from Harry Potter.

Printed in Great Britain
by Amazon